The Incredible Journey of Sterling Vice

Book III in the Raventon Mysteries series

Featuring Taylor Smart and the Raventon Three

A novel by

Mark Randolph Watters

The Raventon Mysteries
Featuring Taylor Smart

Ghosts, some say,
aren't ghosts at all,
that ghosts are people, too.

Sometimes, in times
we least expect,
the past catches up with you.

Sterling Vice and Henry Iverson

Acknowledgements

My humble thanks to Maria (Coker) Ratliff for introducing me to Sterling Vice, an ancestor of hers who participated in, and died during, the American Civil War.

Too little history of the actual Sterling Vice's is known. Official Confederate war records were woefully and regrettably incomplete, many persons and events either not recorded or scantly recorded. Confederate battle accounts came almost entirely from officers' battle reports. Many personal Southern battle and camp-life accounts were captured in soldiers' and citizens' diaries, letters, photographs, and post-war memoirs. The majority of official Confederate records were destroyed in the final weeks of the war, as the Northern noose tightened around strategic Southern locales.

Though his name and some other known facts are used herein, my Sterling Vice character and his deeds are products of my imagination.

My hope is that the real Sterling Vice is depicted here in the respectful, honorable persona I envision him to have been.

ISBN 978-0-359-40620-3

The Incredible Journey of Sterling Vice is a work of fiction. Names, characters, places, and events portrayed in this book, except for historical sites, names, and events, are fictitious and are products of the author's imagination. Any similarity to real persons, living or deceased, is coincidental and not intended by the author.

Printed in the United States of America

For a season, special people come into your life.

Paths intersect. They just do.

You don't know why or for how long.

And then they're gone.

But, you're *better* for them.

"There is no past; there is no future; there is only the present, and its ever-shifting gaggle of props and settings."

-- Sterling Vice --

"Beware of false prophets, which come to you in sheep's clothing, but inwardly they are ravening wolves."

-- Jesus Christ --

For

Kristyn Mikayla Watters,

precious daughter

Author's Notes

Probably more a disclaimer, this note is intended to stress that THE INCREDIBLE JOURNEY OF STERLING VICE could rightly be labeled a "history mystery". It is actually a telling of two stories blended into one, a merging of two plot lines. One plot is set during the third day of the battle of Gettysburg, July, 1863. The second plot is set in contemporary times, specifically 2020, and finds our heroes in their second year of college, home for their summer break.

Then it gets weird.

Reading this novel will require a suspension of disbelief, a setting aside of what you probably know to be true. But isn't that what fiction is? Isn't that precisely what fiction is required to do, at least in some of its aspects? As you read, go with the flow and try not to dwell on any specific points of "fact" or situation. Just accept it for its entertainment value. By all means, please do not take offense. None is intended.

One more thing. In much of the dialogue, I have truncated the letter 'g' in words ending in 'ing', to better reflect contemporaneous speech patterns. You will not see the annoying use of apostrophes to denote that letter's omissions. Dialect can be awkward to express in writing. I've tried not to overuse dialect, annoying as it can be for the reader, though some use is present. I hope it enhances the settings, not annoys the reader.

Mark Randolph Watters

The Incredible Journey of Sterling Vice

Book III in the Raventon Mysteries series

Featuring Taylor Smart and the Raventon Three

A novel by

Mark Randolph Watters

1

Wednesday morning, 11:40
July 3, 1863
Seminary Ridge, Confederate front line
Gettysburg, Pennsylvania

"I don't want you goin out yonder, Charlie," Sterling said, touching the flaming end of a campfire stick to his pipe. He took a long draw and exhaled. "I *mean* it."

"*Why*, Sterling Vice?" Charlie asked.

"You seen what happened yesterday. This'll be *worse*, and this ain't for you, not this time."

"Cain't *nothin* be worse than yesterday," Charlie said. "Ain't for you, neither. Ain't for *none* of us, but I'm stayin with you, Sterling, come what may. Don't try talkin me out of it. Y'all need the cadence of my drum anyhow."

"I s'pect them guns, by the time we get goin 'cross that field, will be all the cadence anybody'll be a-hearin, except maybe the shouts and hollers from their own minds and mouths."

"Only thing that'll push y'all 'cross that field with any kind of order is my little drum here. Ain't that why we exist?"

"You seen what happened at Chancellorsville, Charlie," Sterling said. "When we came out of those woods on them blues, like wolves on mice, the only order was *disorder*."

"You sayin you don't need me, Sterling?"

"We need you, boy. I'm just sayin I don't want to see you killed. An artillery shell burstin don't care a *lick* who it bursts upon."

"Just the same, Sterling, I'm goin with you."

"We'll have the regimental flags; we'll have officers wavin their swords like wild men; we'll have the pride of every man. If that ain't enough to get us across that ground, fear'll make up the difference," Sterling replied, sucking between words on his oak-wood pipe so as to stem its stubborn resistance to the tobacco's burn. "No man wants to be a standin-still target. Don't let 'em catch you standin still."

"I won't, Sterling." Charlie paused and thought. "Hard to b'lieve, ain't it, Sterling?"

"What's that, boy?"

"How *quiet* it is. Midday sun, white cotton clouds. I can hear *birds,* see *squirrels* runnin, dogs barkin, something I ain't noticed for goin on a week now." Charlie looked towards his oblique left, towards the northeast. "All the fightin, all the guns, on the Yankee right have stopped. Cain't hear no more shootin, Sterling. Reckon we whipped 'em yet?"

Sterling took a draw on his pipe and listened. "Reckon we ain't," he figured, cupping his hand around his ear, not noticing the guns' silence until Charlie mentioned it. "Few shots now and again. Ain't hearin no yells of victory. Just means Ewell's men gave it their best, and now it's *our* turn. What time is it?"

Charlie pulled the gold-lidded watch from his pants pocket. "11:45."

Sterling noticed.

"Where'd a young lad like you get such a watch as that? No offense, but that's a right smart timepiece for a twelve-year-old."

"Didn't I show you this somewhere back in Virginia? I'm sure I did. Anyhow, took it off an unburied Yankee, in the woods near Chancellorsville. Had a hole right th'ough his forehead, what was *left* of his forehead anyhow. I s'pect he didn't need it no more, the watch, that is, his time on this earth havin run its course." Charlie smiled at the clever acknowledgement of his acquisition.

"Wow," Sterling said, "it has a *glow* about it. You been polishin it?"

"Every chance I get," Charlie replied with a proud upward tilt of his head and a gleaming smile across his face. "Since I found this here watch, Sterling, seems like whatever I do, I feel a little better, a little stronger. Reckon this watch has some sort of powers?"

"I don't s'pect it's that. A watch is a watch. Tells us the time and how much of it we're wastin. Might it be because you've cleaned it so much, a boy's pride bein what it is?"

"Maybe. My spoil of war, I reckon. Funny thing about this watch, Sterling."

"*Funny* thing? How so?"

Sterling took the watch, its double-lidded case hanging from a double-Albert, from Charlie's hand and examined it. 'Columbia Watch Co' and 'New York' adorned its face between which was hand-painted in elegant red script, "Joseph O. Neal", ostensibly the dead Yankee's name. Black Roman numerals circled the watch's cream-white face. Swirls of fancy engravings framed an etched sailing ship on the watch's back cover, the actual boat perhaps belonging to Neal.

"Ever since I found it, I feel like *nothin* can hurt me, like nothin can *kill* me. I feel like … I can live *forever.*"

"You're just baskin in your ill-gotten riches, boy. No, I reckon he *didn't* need it," Sterling agreed, handing the watch back to Charlie, "not for time-tellin anyhow. You should've put it back in his pocket."

"Ill-gotten? Why, Sterling? He had no more use of it. B'sides, it might not have been his."

"But you said that--"

"Well, truth be told, the watch was layin on the ground 'tween *two* dead Yankees. Fell out of a pocket of one of 'em, you think? Could've belonged to either one, maybe neither. You never know about these things, Sterling, and well, since I had no way o' tellin, I kep' it for myself. If his shoes weren't already taken, I'd-a grabbed them, too."

"Reckon *one* of them two boys had *one* final use of it. Bad luck to take a dead soldier's belongings. Like robbin a grave. Now no one'll ever know the name that went with the body. Spoils of war, yes, but anonymity is a horrible way to exit this life, boy, an' *somebody's* name, even if it ain't your own, is better'n no name at all."

"Ano ... anomyn ...".

"Means he'll go through eternity as an unknown soldier, unless his family is fortunate enough to find and identify him. Keep yourself safe, boy. Don't let that watch become someone *else's* spoils of war."

"I won't. I wonder who this Joseph O. Neal fellow is," Charlie asked.

2

"I was wonderin the same thing. That name has a familiar ring to it. Seems I've heard it before. Did you see the cover lid, Charlie, *inside* the cover lid?"

"See what, Sterling?"

"Take a look," Sterling said.

Charlie opened the lid. Inside, inscribed in relief gold was 'Isaiah 48:9'.

"What's Isaiah 48:9, Sterling?"

"Old Testament scripture. I don't know the passage. Must have been important to Mister Joseph O. Neal."

"I'm still goin with you, Sterling," Charlie said, closing the lid and dropping the watch into his pocket.

"I know you are. Ain't gon' try to stop you. Be like tryin to stop a bullet with a biscuit. But you stay behind me the whole time, you understand?"

"Sterling, I can't b'lieve what we went th'ough yesterday," Charlie said, eyes fixed on the open field to their front, "what we witnessed … what we … survived."

"Thought about that all night, Charlie." Sterling sighed and rested his back against a sycamore tree. He pulled his rifle across his lap and gave his pipe a smokeless draw. "Saw things yesterday I thought I'd *never* see in all my days. Men's heads blown off, arms and legs shot to pieces, men fallin next to me, in front of me, on top of me. Noise so loud, a man couldn't hear himself yell, never mind hearin a *drum's* roll. Looked and sounded like the very end of the world. Of course, for a lot of boys, it was *exactly* that."

Sterling paused for a reflective moment and continued. Charlie listened.

"Flags wavin, droppin, risin. Explodin shells sendin men flyin, like twigs in a breeze. Wounded men, bleedin men, cryin like helpless babies for their wives, their mamas, their children, reachin out to anything they could grab hold of.

"Men cursin at every step, oaths hurled faster'n bullets. Blood everywhere, puddles on rocks, in the dirt, drippin off green grass and amber wheat, splattered all over my shirt and pants. Devil's playground. Wasn't a lick of order to it, men loadin and shootin, not *aimin*, just firin', tryin to knock out of the air whatever bullet might be comin at 'em, knock down whatever of the enemy might be in their fronts."

Sterling and Charlie sat silently for a few pensive moments, still absorbing the shock, each no more than a stitch in the long Confederate thread of men to their right and left, thousands of others staring into the strangely quiet early afternoon air heating up like a rising crescendo, each man fully aware these precious hours of life might well be their last.

"You … you *kill* anybody yesterday, Sterling?" Charlie asked in reference to yesterday's back-and-forth bloodletting in a Pennsylvania wheat field.

Sterling looked away, gathering his thoughts to justify his actions in that wheat field, as if justification were necessary.

He had often preached the virtues of the Ten Commandments to his family and friends back home, not the least of which was number six. Sin was sin, whether or not framed by the context of war, Sterling knew, and forgiveness could only come from God.

"Didn't want to, Charlie," he replied, eyes focused on the open expanse of the grassy field out front and its gradual rise toward the enemy's line a mile off, "and God forgive me for it. But I likely did, I'm pretty sure. Thought it might be a bit easy, like killin an intruder back home, a scavenger tryin to take what ain't rightly his, a man causin harm to my family, my actions bein all in the interest of self-defense. But those Yankees had the same fears as me. They were followin orders, same as me, aimin with their mouths open an' shootin with their eyes closed, throwin their lives into a maelstrom they had no control over, each prayin he'd come out alive. Same as me. Shoot or be shot. And then the killin became easy."

"*Easy?* Killin was *easy* for you?"

"Not the takin-of-life part of killin, but the *defendin* part. Had no choice, Charlie, none of us did. Had a line of Yankees chargin me, chargin *all* of us. Scariest damn thing I ever experienced, a mass of screamin, armed humanity closin down on me, bullets flyin all around me. All I could think about was my family, my wife and young-uns, and how I was ever goin to live to see 'em again. I pulled the trigger as I dodged first one Yankee bayonet and then another. Didn't see him no more, but the smoke was thick all over. Maybe he ran past me; maybe he fell dead. Couldn't see much of anything. Just kep' loadin and firin, loadin and firin, fast as swattin at a swarm of bees. Instinct's what it was. I fired a bunch of rounds … into a *bunch* of men … or what I *thought* was men. Might've been no more'n clouds of smoke, stumps of trees. No time to note the difference or the results."

Sterling paused and sighed.

"Sure didn't like the thought of killin anyone, Charlie. No, sirree, not one bit. But I had no luxury of time in that swirl to ponder the idea."

Charlie considered Sterling's words. "Think you'll kill somebody today?"

"Reckon so, reckon we *all* will, maybe even *you* will, assumin we get anywhere close to that line out yonder. I don't know how God'll take a view of this war, all this killin, Charlie. All I can say is thankfully we're under Grace now, not law."

"Can we take that ridge yonder, Sterling?"

Sterling gazed a moment toward the Yankee line.

"I ain't sayin we won't or cain't, Charlie." Sterling struck a match to his shoe and touched the flame to his stubborn tobacco. "But if you want my honest opinion--"

"I *do*, Sterling. I do."

Sterling sighed. "We ain't got the chance of a mouse in a den of lions, boy. For a right good many of us, today's our last day on earth."

"Whose side is God on, anyhow?"

"Well, Charlie," Sterling said, pausing as he spoke, grappling for an answer to a question that defied answers, drawing on the clog of tobacco as the flame caught, "I think God only takes the side of Holiness. Hard to imagine war being holy. But Mr. Lincoln has taken a Holy approach by freein the slaves and makin this war about Union *and* freedom for the negros. That just might give God and the Yankees the edge."

"Do you think God's no more'n a *spectator* in this war?"

"Could be, Charlie. Could be. Prob'bly cryin His eyes out over it, too. I think maybe God's lettin our free-will and our human limitations guide the course of this war, and thus the outcome of this war."

Sterling paused to take a sip of precious water from his canteen. He offered the vessel to Charlie.

"Reckon prayer amounts to anything, then?" Charlie asked as he turned the canteen to his mouth and swallowed. He coughed, wiping his mouth with the back of a hand. "In this war, that is, for the South?"

"I reckon it does. God still loves you, all of us, even those who pull the triggers, regardless of side. Just pray for *God's* will to override *your* will, Charlie, and remember *He's* in control, come what may."

"But our will, our intention, is to kill the enemy. That God's will, too?"

"God's will, I believe, is that the war *end*, that all men are *free*, that Americans *unite* in His name. But it's also God's will not to force those righteous things on us. Whatever the outcome, God's Will be done in the end, according to His plan."

"Thanks, Sterling." Charlie took more water and swallowed. "I like to think your words are just what my daddy might have said."

Sterling smiled and patted Charlie on the head.

3

"Just a little of that water, mind you," Sterling said as he wiped the flow of sweat from his forehead. "It's got to last."

"Might *be* my last." Charlie managed two more quick swallows before handing the canteen back to Sterling. He stared at Sterling.

"What is it, Charlie?"

"Just wonderin ... You afraid to die, Sterling?"

"Used to be afraid. A lot. I think now I'm more afraid of *sufferin*. I guess any man who *ain't* afraid is a fool, human nature being what it is. But I ain't *as* afraid, not anymore, not after what we did and seen yesterday. Jesus, forgive us our killin ways," Sterling said, his eyes turned skyward.

"Looked like some of them fellers, ours too, were enjoyin it a bit *too* much," Sterling continued. "I have to admit I took some joy in seein those men fall. A man gets caught up in the rush of survivin.

"Can't think much about it now, all this killin, about me or you dyin. I'll think about it later, under a sunset, smokin a pipe, listening to a whippoorwill. It's going to happen sooner or later, dyin, and there ain't a bit we can do about it.

"Thinkin about it won't help none. Ain't got that luxury, not now, and I don't b'lieve I *care* to have that luxury. I s'pose it's times like this that folks refer to when sayin it's easier to ask forgiveness, for our killin one another, that is, than to get permission."

"What?" Charlie asked, scratching his scalp. "I thought Jeff Davis and Marse Robert done *gave* us that permission."

"Never you mind. Theirs, Lincoln's and Meade's, too, are burdens we can never know, thank God. All these men here, on both sides, will do what they have to do, what they're told to do. Our boys'll do their duty, or die tryin, just as them boys in blue'll do theirs."

"Don't sound fair, Sterling," Charlie said. "They got more soldiers, more equipment, more food ..."

Sterling removed his hat and wiped away the relentless slide of sweat from his forehead to his eyes and down his face. He placed his hand on his canteen but resisted the temptation.

"Hotter'n *blazes* out here. All I know, Charlie, is they ain't *nothin* fair 'bout *none* of this, for *nobody*. I can only place the outcomes in God's hands and pray for the comfort and understanding of my family back home."

"I'm part of your family, too, right, Sterling?"

"Sure thing, partner." Sterling smiled.

4

"I hear tell they gon' send us 'cross that field there," said a soldier walking up to Sterling's left, pointing as he spoke, droplets of sweat glistening and gliding along undulations of crevices carved into his forehead by long days spent in the driving sunlight and by his own personal experiences of battle. Gooey black powder smeared his face. His hatless hair glistened wet, strands fused like matted straw. "After Porter Alexander shells them out of existence, that is."

"I hear we're the only *fresh* troops Lee's got, at least *y'all* are, that is," Sterling replied, his gaze fixed forward across the broad expanse of grass and ground.

"What do you mean *'y'all'*," replied the soldier. "Ain't you one of *us?*"

"What I mean is, you're part of *Pickett's* division, brought up from the reserves, for this very fight. I was with McClaw's division, Georgians; fought over that way yesterday," Sterling noted, pointing.

"How'd you get detached from your unit?" the soldier asked.

"Damned if I know. Lucky to be alive."

"D'pends on what you call *'fresh'*," the soldier said, propping his hands atop his rifle barrel. "Most of these fellows are with Pickett, but I fought with Anderson, 7th Georgia, yesterday ev'nin. Ain't had a decent night's sleep in goin on *two years*, an' I'm livin off belly fat, what little they's left of it."

Sterling reached into his haversack, this item picked from the ground yesterday during hasty maneuvers around the wheat field fight. He retrieved three overripe, bruised peaches he had gathered in an adjacent peach orchard. "Here you go," he said, turning and handing them to the soldier. "Ain't much, but they're better'n noth - *Hey!* I know *you!* I *know* you! *Henry Iverson,* you ol' *hound dog,* you!"

The two gripped each other in a hug, slapping backs.

"*Lots* better'n nothin. Thanks," Henry said, taking the peaches. "Thought that was you. Seen you from a few hundred feet away and thought I'd stroll over to confirm. Much obliged for the peaches, Sterling Vice," Iverson replied, smiling a knowing smile, taking the peaches and consuming them in a few seconds, spitting out the pits as might a Spencer repeater spit bullets. Droplets of peach juice dampened his trousers like a spring shower. "Even the fuzz's good."

The two hugged again, entangled in a few fleeting moments of homegrown comfort.

"Speakin of fuzz, I hardly recognized you with your beard," Sterling said as he took a closer look into Iverson's eyes. "So, you rascal, since when did you join a *Virginia* regiment?" Sterling asked.

"Since this mornin, I reckon. Lost contact with my own Georgia bunch; ended up here, with Pickett."

"What do you think about this, what we're about to do, that is?" Sterling asked.

"Ain't you gon' introduce me, Sterling?" Charlie interrupted, staring at the tall, muscular Iverson.

"Iverson's the name, young man. Henry Iverson."

"Pleased to know you, Mr. Iverson. Charlie's my name."

"Call me Henry. Where you from, Charlie," Iverson asked. Mighty fine-lookin drum you got there."

"Thanks. Oh, a little bit of everywhere. Make my home now in Raventon, Georgia, I reckon, such as I'm able to rightfully call a place home. I s'pose home's where you tap your drum." Charlie smiled.

"Got a last name, Charlie?"

"Reckon I do; just cain't remember it."

Henry looked at Sterling and gave a half smile. "Well … ain't you a might *young* for this? Do your folks know you're here?"

"My folks don't care one way or another. Ain't got no folks. So here I be."

"Raventon, Georgia, you say? Yes sir, know it well. Lived there a while myself. Some of my family's still there. Had me a young lady friend from up around Raventon once upon a time," Henry said, glancing toward Sterling. "Elizabeth was her name."

"Once upon a time? What *happened* to her," Charlie asked.

"Married ol' Sterling here," Iverson replied laughing, swatting Sterling on the back. "Water under the bridge.

"As for what I think of what we're about to do, Sterling – as if what I think matters a wit in this war -- we're about to commit *suicide,* is what we're about to do. Ain't no two ways about it."

"I think you're right, Henry," Sterling agreed, wiping away with his forearm the ceaseless assaults of sweat. "Only way out of this is to *run*, I reckon. An' ain't *none* of us gon' run, us *or* them."

"Well, I'll tell you, Sterling, I know what you mean, but runnin might be the only *sensible* thing to do. That yonder ain't nothin but a *fool's game,*" Henry replied, pointing. "Longstreet's boys got all the way up the crest of that ridge yonder, yesterday ev'nin. I *know.* I was amongst 'em, with the 7th Georgia, Anderson's brigade. Even saw direc'ly into the rear of the Yankee line, a regular ocean of blue waitin on us, but then we got no support. *No* support, I tell you. I heard A.P. Hill was supposed to send up a brigade. Wouldn't have been enough, I reckon, but it would have been *moral* support at least."

Henry sighed. "We had 'em in our grasp an' let 'em go. So, we gon' make that *same* mistake twice, and on consecutive days? My money's on 'yes, we are'. Lee's blood is up, an' they ain't no turnin back now. Support's what we need, only it ain't what we're gettin. And without it … we can't take that ridge." Iverson shook his head and spat.

He continued. "Support is the one thing we seem to lack in this army. Exterior lines stretched thinner'n a bad excuse, we are. We make a *grand* fight, take what we fight for, but we cain't *hold* it. No, sir, don't like the looks of this at all."

"Diff'rent this time around, boy," said another soldier, as he overheard the conversation, his back pressed against a birch tree, hat slouched over his forehead, a short stem of dry wheat dangling from his lips, as if he were settled in for an afternoon nap, as if this whole business of assaulting enemy lines were as routine as hardtack, green corn, and bad water.

"Different? How so?" Iverson asked.

"Pendleton's got all his artill'ry strung out far as the eye can see," the soldier replied, waving his arm in a 180-degree arc. "Over a hunnerd pieces, I'd say; maybe a lot *more*. Cain't see 'em all for them trees down that way, but they're there. Gon' soften up their lines, take out some of their guns, *make way* for the infantry, for you an' me. Gettin all the support we need *here*, from these iron-spittin devils, in *advance* of the main attack. They'll advance the guns as the men advance the lines."

"You sound awfully confident," Sterling said, stuffing his pipe with bits of shredded corn shucks he had packed into his haversack. "We'll see about that. All them guns' firin, ours *and* theirs, will make it right hard for anybody to see what they're hittin. We'll see."

"An' *me!*" Charlie insisted with a soft tap of his drum. "Makin way for *me*, too! Got to have the cadence of the drummers."

"Maybe so, son, but this affair ain't for you, lest you yearnin to become shell fodder. Trouble is," Iverson observed, "we got us a long march 'cross that field, fences to climb, to knock down, worse than what Burnside had at Fredericksburg. An' we know what we done to *those* boys. No, sir, I ain't likin the looks of this little adventure one bit. We *had* 'em day b'fore yesterday and yesterday, too. We didn't take advantage of opportunities, and, well, here we are." He turned to Sterling, studying his face. "You new to this war, Mr. Vice?"

"Sort of, I reckon," Sterling replied. "Depends on how you define 'new'. When did you enlist, April of '61, was it?"

"Early May, '61. Walked all the way to Atlanta to do it. New regiments were formin just about all over the place. How about you?"

"We got here a week ago, Charlie an' me. Walked for two months from Wedowee to Raventon and up to here, by way of the Blue Ridge Mountains and through Richmond.

"As for time served, yes, I'm newer than tomorrow's sunrise, but, experience-wise ... feels like a lifetime already. Made Chancellorsville on the second day of that fight and didn't do a lot of shootin beyond carryin Hooker's right flank, but I seen the field. Bodies all over the ground. A glorious victory for General Lee; a terrible cost for the armies."

"Indeed it was," Iverson said. "Sure could use Jackson right about now. If Stonewall was here, we wouldn't be fightin this third-day. It would already have been decided by now. That's what Ewell's men have been up to all mornin, tryin to take what should've been took day before yesterday."

"I hear you, Henry."

"Say, no wonder you're so lean, walkin all that way. How're the folks back in Wedowee? I write when I can, but I don't get no replies."

"They write me every now and again. S'pect I'll see a letter or two direc'ly. Lots of mail, outbound *and* inbound, gets lost, I figure. I did see some of your letters to them; theirs to you, too, back home b'fore I come up. No doubt the mail ain't gettin through fast as it ought. It'll catch up with us direc'ly. How'd you end up in the 38th Virginia?" Sterling asked.

"*38th Virginia?* So *that's* why these boys talk so funny," Iverson whispered, smiling. "Like I said, I was originally with the 7th Georgia. Don't know where those boys ended up. Dead on the field, many of 'em, I s'pect. Did some gosh-awful fightin back yonder ways," Iverson said, pointing to their right towards a patch of woods, Rose's Woods, "yesterday in a field of wheat, I think it was. Hard to tell with all the tramplin and bleedin just what sort of field it was."

"*Battle* field," Sterling said, puffing on his pipe. "The *battlest* of fields."

5

"Yep. Next to us was a bunch of boulders, bigger'n houses, men fallin everywhere. Devil's Den, I hear it's called, them boulders. Texans and Alabamians tried pushin hard to take a timber-cleared hill, Little Round Top's its name, but failed. No support. Same ol' story. All of us were so dang exhausted, all that marchin just gettin here, sun beatin down, chargin hills under fire, no water. Hot as the devil, too, an' it was a *devil* of a spot to be in. Bullets whistlin and screamin like the hounds of hell itself." Iverson paused for a moment of marveling. "Yet, here I am to tell of it. To God be the glory!

"We took them boulders, drivin off a battery of artill'ry. Next thing I know, I'm being rallied by some colonel into the 7th Georgia's line formin to attack across that field yonder, that *very same* field we're about to march through now. We made it up that little ridge on the horizon there -- see it, next to that patch of trees -- right up to their line, an' we seen *smack* into the Promised Land, the rear of the mighty Potomac Army itself.

"Again, no support. Lucky to get back to the line's starting point, back across fought-for land. Fell in with Pickett's division this morning. I s'pect a lot of men are separated from their units. But a rifle's a rifle, needed no matter where on the line that rifle is firin. So, how'd *you* wind up in a Virginia regiment?"

"Well," replied Sterling, "I'm no mustered-in member of any regiment, so they threw me in with the 11th Georgia day before yesterday, Colonel Little's regiment, part of Anderson's brigade. Seen some heavy fightin myself in a wheat field yesterday – same one you was in, I'm sure -- near that same Little Round Top hill and the boulders you spoke of. Most incredible thing I ever seen, lines surgin back an' forth, men goin down like tater-filled canvas sacks, blood splatterin on the dirt like red rain.

Death's celebration. I marvel that any man made it out alive, unhit.

"I thought surely I was a goner, makin all sorts of promises to God if He would just *get me through* that swirl of death."

"What'd you promise, Sterling?" asked Charlie.

"Little o' this, little o' that," Sterling replied. "That I'd get you home alive. Thank the Lord, He got us through. Got separated in all the fray, an' Charlie an' me ended up here, with this unit, with y'all. Pickett's division, is what I'm told." Sterling lowered his voice to a whisper and smiled. "Funny-talkin Virginians."

"Well, now, *that's* what I call a baptism by fire," Iverson said. "Sounds like you had it at least as rough as me. Wish you'd been with *me* at Chancellorsville. Whipped 'em at Hazel Grove and again at Fairview, pushin 'em back from the crossroads of Chancellorsville to plum near the Rapidan, like stray dogs. We almost done the same thing late yesterday. Came *this* close. Devil of a spot to be in, especially not to be able to close the door on them boys."

"From the looks and sounds of it all, don't reckon there's any spot what *ain't* a devil of a spot. Dead and wounded *everywhere*, theirs and ours. This is one *hell* of a fight, an' the fun's just begun."

"Truth told, brother," Iverson agreed. "Beats all I ever seen at Chancellorsville, even at Sharpsburg. An' I'm afraid we're next."

"Except for divine intervention, I don't rightly know how I missed bein shot, bullets flyin thicker'n skeeters at a swamp party. Look here," Sterling said, taking off his hat and inserting a finger into a jagged opening near its top. "A bullet took it right off my noggin, missed taking me out of this life by a frog's hair. Spared me for one more day at least. Grazed my scalp. Still stings."

"Count your blessins, man, while your lungs can breathe the words," Iverson advised. "Today just might balance things out. If not today, tomorrow or the next.

"Say you cain't remember your last name, Charlie?" Henry prodded.

"It's *Dyer*, Henry," Sterling said, a huff of frustration in his voice. "He just wants you to pay him some attention's, all."

"Aw, why'd you have to go an' *tell* him, Sterling! Cain't a man have *something* of a mystery to hisself?"

Iverson chuckled. "Pleasure to know you, Charlie … what was it? Dwyer? Dunhill?" he replied as he took measure of the boy. "But don't you worry none. I'm pretty good at forgettin stuff, so ask me in a while an' I *guarantee* you your last name will be long forgotten by me. You're talkin to a man who cain't remember his *own* last name, much less somebody else's. Besides, a man's *entitled* to some mystery."

"Hmmm. I like you, Mr. Iverson," Charlie said with a smile after a moment's ponder. "First time anybody's suggested I was a *man*."

Iverson smiled and patted Charlie's shoulder.

6

"Get ready to give the long roll, Charlie," Sterling noted, the field's deafening silence rising to a crescendo of calm, "'cause it's 'bout that time."

"How do you know, Sterling?" Charlie asked.

"Feel it in my bones, boy. Feels like all this silence is *beggin* for an explosion."

"My bones, too." Iverson pulled up a stem of wheat and raised himself from a birch tree lean-to, grabbed his rifle, and gave a sigh. "Need to stretch my legs. Give or take an hour, we'll be marchin straight into the teeth of hell. If our aims are true, and theirs *ain't* ... we might just see suppertime. If not, well ... so, what time is it?"

Charlie produced his pocket watch, opening it. "12:58."

"That's a right nice timepiece you got there, boy," Iverson said.

"Thanks," Charlie replied. I get a lot of attention from soldiers and officers when they see this watch. Why, General Longstreet hisself asked me the time yesterday. Seen me polishing it. Came right up and asked me. Colonel Alexander, too. General Longstreet said he'd trade me his spurs for it. Now, what's a drummer boy gon' do with *spurs*, I asked him." Charlie smiled.

"Shaw!" Sterling said, "Longstreet asked you that? Now I *know* you're lyin!"

"I just bet you do get a lot of attention with that watch. But, like your last name, you might want to keep that watch a mystery, too."

"*Now* I remember!" Sterling shouted.

"Remember *what?*" Charlie replied.

"Who that Joseph O. Neal fellow is?"

"Joseph O. Neal?" Iverson asked.

"Right here," Charlie answered, showing Iverson the watch again. "Name's painted on the face."

"He was a well-known Pennsylvania preacher, said to have had the powers of healing, even *resurrection.*"

"Resurrection?" Iverson said. "I thought that was the exclusive providence of Christ, of God Almighty."

"Maybe Christ delegates from time to time," Sterling offered.

"But ... *resurrection*?"

"What they say. Said he brought a whole company of Yankee soldiers *back to life* after Sharpsburg. I never b'lieved a word of it. So, that's *Joseph O. Neal's* watch, eh?"

No wonder I feel so good with this watch, Charlie thought. *I got the resurrection in me!*

He smiled and shoved the timepiece back into his pocket, looking as he did so to see if he and the watch might have been noticed by others along the line. "I always do," Charlie said, "keep it a mystery, that is, an' -- *Look!*"

7

Colonel Edward Porter Alexander, field commander of Lee's artillery, pulled reins on his horse, slinging a cloud of dust forward as he stopped near General Longstreet, commander of Lee's First Corps, who straddled a fence at the tree line behind Armistead's brigade. Longstreet turned slowly toward Alexander, who lifted himself erect in his stirrups, anxious for the word to begin the bombardment of the Union defenses.

"Hey, *Charlie,*" Alexander said. "Got the time?"

"See what I mean," Charlie whispered, wisking the watch from his pocket. "1:01, sir."

Sterling and Iverson stared wide-eyed at each other, jaws dropped.

"Thank you, son. Any minute now, sir," Alexander said, giving notice that all the guns were in place and ready to commence the bombardment.

"Thank you, Colonel," said Longstreet. "You know, yesterday's fight was the finest three hours of fighting any army, anytime, has ever done."

"Yes, sir, indeed it was."

"Alexander *knows* you, Charlie?" Henry asked, stunned by this latest.

"Yep. He and I go all the way back to yesterday," Charlie replied with a prideful grin.

Alexander had arrayed some one hundred and sixty-three cannon in an irregular, convex, mile-long arc, their aims concentrating on the center of Cemetery Ridge, three-quarters of a mile forward of the Confederates on Seminary Ridge. The morning's haze had lifted. Cicadas echoed the building heat. Black-barreled Parrott rifles and bronze Napoleons flattened the grasses of the field in their path of the arc, their aims set, their barrels filled with solid shot and explosive shells, the high sun sending flashes of blinding light reflecting off those barrels.

"You may commence firing when ready, Colonel."

"Yes, sir."

Three cannon shots exploded in swift succession, the signal for the remaining one hundred and sixty cannons to do the same, the beginning of a two-hour artillery sling, Lee's last-gasp plan to soften, if not dislodge, Union artillery and infantry, paving the way for an infantry assault on the Union center.

Men stood, palms covering their ears, craning their necks to not only hear history but to bear witness to this most intense and massive artillery barrage, the greatest that the war -- and the continent -- had ever witnessed. Others climbed trees to maximize and to clarify their views, despite Union shells whining overhead and slicing through those same trees.

Charlie pressed his palms against his ears, a futile attempt to muzzle the thunderous growl of the guns.

Union artillery joined the fight. Shells screamed past, exploding on the reverse slope of Seminary

Ridge, yet still within killing range of standing Confederates.

"Get down, Charlie!" shouted Sterling. "*Stay* down!"

Showers of dirt and stone swept the line of rebels. Shrapnel of white-hot iron cut through branches, sending death and injury from places three dimensional.

The air dripped thick with early-afternoon humidity, brushing the guns' output with yellow-white strokes of color, scores of belching cannon sending swaths of flame propelling the smoke and iron, like rabid dragons. Summer leaves wobbled loose from branches and curled earthward on paths of vibration, their peaceful decent a counterpoint to the encompassing violence. The very ground seemed to shake.

As they readied the guns for subsequent shots, artillerymen strained to see through the smoke the impacts of their missiles. Eyes winced with each blast, cannon after cannon leaping upward and backward. Crews wrestled their guns back into place and repeated the process.

Sterling rolled his sleeves above his elbows and sat against a thick oak tree, shielding himself, he hoped, from exploding enemy shells. Charlie and Henry Iverson joined him.

"You learn fast, Sterling," Iverson observed.

"No sense giving the Yankees our lives without a fight, without a shot, and anyway, ain't nothing to do but wait," Sterling answered. "Just hope a falling branch doesn't impale me."

Every man in line behind the row of guns knew what was coming. They had been placed here, below the ridgeline out of plain sight, for a singular purpose. The fate of these three days of battle now rested with these men, thousands already having set the bloodstained table in the two and a half days prior.

The artillery was just the prelude, this afternoon's opening stanza to the macabre poetry of battle. Men paced about to Sterling's left and right, heads ducking instinctively with each belch of a gun. Some craned their necks to see over the ridgeline ahead, trees and shrubs, soldiers and smoke, blocking any clear view. Others made their ways toward the tree line, despite officers' orders to stay put, to the stretch of open field before them, to view as best they could the battle line they would be asked to assault, to take.

Some sat, scraps of paper pressed against their thighs, against their Bibles, against their friends' backs, stubs of pencils hurriedly scratching out letters home, last words stuffed into their pockets, words offering a measure of comfort to the eventual readers and to the writers alike.

Sterling scribbled some quick words, dating it "July 3, 1863 in some field in Pennsylvania", quickly giving the message to an orderly collecting such for ultimate delivery to waiting eyes homeward. Every soldier considered these their last words to loved ones.

Veterans ignored the mayhem sent forth by the guns, instead playing cards or warming coffee over hastily constructed campfires. These men had fought on the front lines of Second Manassas and Sharpsburg and Fredericksburg and Chancellorsville. Nothing

Gettysburg could throw at them would convince them they had not already seen the worst of the Elephant and thus had already experienced this war's worst. If death was at hand, so be it. They had survived those battles; they would survive this. Or not.

A soldier handed Sterling a tin cup of steaming coffee, the fine powdery grounds confiscated from a pouch inside the haversack of a dead Yankee a month ago in the Wilderness near Chancellorsville.

"Thank you," Sterling replied, taking the cup. "Why for me?"

"Why *not* for you?" the soldier replied. "You look like you need it."

"I do at that."

The minutes passed painfully, like a million small cuts, no one knowing if the present minute might be his last.

8

"You're new at this, aincha?" the soldier asked, grinning, spitting tobacco juice and sipping his coffee. "Ain't no shame in that."

"That obvious, is it, my newness?" Sterling asked.

"You got that look, like you might've been through this before but not confident enough to ignore your fears."

"First big battle. Well, I was at Chancellorsville, but I didn't get there in time to do much. Here's different. Seen and done all I care to see and do, truth be told."

"I was at Chancellorsville, too," Iverson replied to the soldier, part of Jackson's flank attack, A.P. Hill's division."

"You boys pushed that Union right flank plum out of the fight. Good work. Mighty good work. Too bad about Jackson."

"I was afraid then," Iverson said. "Afraid now, too. You're *not* afraid?"

"As a mouse in a field full of cats," the soldier admitted. "But, either I'll live or I'll die, and only God controls those outcomes. Ain't no use worryin about it."

"Looks to me like them Yankees might have a say in that, too," Sterling replied.

The soldier smiled. "Means to an end, if God wills. I've seen men live through sheets of bullets thicker'n mad hornets, unscathed. I've seen men picked off by sharpshooters a mile away. Battles are strange, fickle. Ain't nothin certain till it happens."

"You could get wounded, sent home."

"Rather be killed outright than wounded," the soldier replied. "If you weren't new at this, you'd know that."

"From what I've seen, I'm inclined to agree with you. Hope to avoid a wound. I've seen what a one-ounce ball of lead can do to flesh and bone. Ugly sight."

"Where you from, Johnny?" Iverson asked the soldier.

"Finster's the name. Pap Finster. Richmond way, maybe Lynchburg. Don't rightly know. I *do* know this is my last fight."

"How can you know that?" Sterling asked. "You at the end of your enlistment?"

"No, I still got me a year and a half to go on my commitment. You just know these things, feel 'em." Finster said, gazing stoically across the field, shells bursting and bouncing at every point, sending up waves of soil and stone. "We're about to march into the point of no return, mouth of Satan himself. Experience tells a man when his time's near. My experience screams it. That open field screams it, not to mention those blue bellies lining that ridge yonder, rifles aimed low and straight, cannon barrels stuffed with canister."

"Pap. That your given name?" Iverson asked.

"It's my war-given name. Had it since Manassas, the first one. Because of my gray hair, I reckon." Finster chuckled. "Makes me look older'n most of these bucks."

Then, silence. Confederate guns ceased firing.

Charlie glanced at his pocket watch.

2:55.

Union guns had ceased firing a half hour earlier.

Soldiers' conversations whittled to a halt. Men gathered their rifles in anticipation of the orders to come, laying down their haversacks and other weighty accoutrements unneeded for the task before them.

"It's Elephant time, boys," Finster said as he placed a percussion cap on the hammer's nipple.

9

General George Pickett, seen by Sterling and Iverson riding up to General Longstreet, was heard asking, "Shall we commence the assault, General?"

Longstreet gave no oral reply. He lowered his head, turned, and gave a slight nod, the only signal giving his approval for an attack he had long concluded was futile.

"We shall *take* their lines," Pickett said, sensing his commander's doubts.

"Fall in, 38th Virginia!" shouted the regiment's captain. Captains up and down the line repeated the order.

Sterling dropped his haversack and bedroll next to an ancient oak, the bark green and wet with his and

Charlie's initials he had carved during some pensive moments overnight. He stood to relieve himself and stooped to retrieve his rifle leaning low against a stone.

Sterling, joined by Finster, Charlie, and Henry, trotted toward the line forming thirty yards to their front. Sterling turned back as if to make sure those items were still there at that tree, that they were real, waiting like puppies for his return.

Saluting, Pickett yanked his reins, turning his horse ninety degrees left, eastward, trotting into the open field in front of the tree line marking Seminary Ridge and his parade-aligned Virginia regiments.

The men stood silent, straight as pines, rifles held vertical by their right hands, against their right shoulders, eyes forward, awaiting their commander's words. Each man, reaching deep into his well of courage, conducted his own personal vigil of prayer and remembrance, knowing *this* was their moment of truth.

Raising his sword and lifting his frame, standing in his stirrups, he gave the command. "Up men, and to your posts! Remember that today … you are from *Old Virginia!"*

Sterling smiled, not sure he ought to agree with those words. He thought of his wife, Betty, and sons, George, Amos, Calvin, and Charles and the hundreds of miles that separated them, Raventon from Gettysburg, just as the screech of an enemy shell tore through branches high overhead.

Instinctively, soldiers flinched; the impulse denied in the face of the enemy to abandon their discipline and to shield their heads with their arms, as limbs and leaves showered their positions, standing now a few yards forward of the afflicted line of woods. Yankee artillery began their long-range response at the sight of these Confederate legions arrayed for attack.

10

"First fight, Sterling?" Finster asked.

"Not if you count yesterday. And maybe Chancellorsville."

More enemy shells screamed their arrival up and down the Confederate line, shattering treetops.

"Was in a little scrape yesterday a bit south of here, in some open ground of wheat and boulders. Say folks around here call that place Devil's Den. Sure was hell t' pay, all right."

"I was right there with you. I heard some Alabamians and Texans tried to take a little hill across the low ground from them boulders. Couldn't take it. Bad omen."

Haversacks, bedrolls, scatterings of tin cups and canteens, playing cards and dice, even rifle cartridges,

dotted the ground and against that same tree, as well as other trees left and right along the mile-long line. Sterling strained to distinguish his own, to no avail, as the items, many destined to become souvenirs and relics, blended into one mass amid the roiling smoke.

"Find 'em when I get back, I reckon," he mumbled. "If I get back."

"Up men, and to your posts!" Pickett was heard to shout again from atop his horse somewhere down the line. "Don't forget that today, you are from *Old Virginia!"*

Cheers pierced the swollen, putrid air. Hats in hands, raised high in that air, waved liked a frantic, rolling sea of patriotism. Individuals became bonded units, each man fully aware death waited ahead, but wholly expectant the Reaper would favor not him but another man, and that the glory of success would envelop their noble efforts and embellish the tales they fancied telling their children and grandchildren.

"Fix bayonets!" shouted captains.

The crisp rustle, the clanking of thirteen thousand moving muskets and bayonets, signaled the moment was at hand.

"On my command! Forward, *march!*"

Twenty-six thousand feet, some with shoes taken from their fallen enemy, others barefoot for months, shuffled forth, like summer thunder.

11

"What's that you said, Finster?" Iverson asked, his musket rested against his right shoulder.

"Said? What'd I say?" Finster replied. And where's *your* bayonet?"

"Somewhere between here and Chambersburg. You said somethin 'bout *findin* somethin."

"I did?" Finster stood silent, thoughtful, eyes straight ahead, smoke twisting across the vast open ground, silhouettes of soldiers and horses and artillery moving on that ridge across that hellish expanse. Horses galloped parallel to the Confederate line, couriers delivering dispatches of orders.

"Oh, yeah. So I did."

"So, what did you *say*, man?"

"Shaw, it ain't nothin important. You'd just laugh."

"Won't laugh if you don't want me to. But I could use a good laugh right about now."

"I ain't never been *saved*, Iverson," Finster confessed.

"Saved from *what?*" Henry replied, half-listening.

"From Satan's hell. I ain't never opened my heart to Jesus. I ain't never asked forgiveness for my share of sins. Figured I wouldn't need to for a while yet. Figured I'd live forever. Too late now."

"Long as you got a breath in your lungs, ain't never too late for that. Hell's right across that field. We all know it. Ain't none of us liable to get saved from that. But you still *can* get saved from that other hell, that *eternal* hell."

Finster nodded and turned his gaze to the ground ahead, wind-waved grass ahead of the lines of Confederates and the ridge that was the objective. Artillery shells arced and screamed overhead.

"I miss my family, my little girl. I want to see-- You believe in divine intervention?" Finster asked.

"I do. But there're some things the Lord just steps away from, let's us sort out for ourselves. This here attack feels exactly like one of those things."

Finster closed his eyes and released a sigh.

"But if you're lookin for Jesus's salvation from hell's side of *eternity,*" Sterling said, overhearing the conversation, "then I reckon you best get to prayin. Time is not on your side. We need undistracted soldiers *now*, so get it done."

"Doin just that," Finster said, one eye open. "Jesus, I am the chiefest among sinners, chiefer, I reckon, than Paul himself. If I don't make it out of this, if I am struck down by an enemy bullet, please forgive –"

At that moment, another order was given.

"Guide left *oblique!*" shouted Colonels at irregular intervals along the line.

Twenty-six thousand shoes and bare feet issued a gush of thunder, like all the world's sandpaper on a mighty forest. Sterling, Finster, and Iverson, shoulder to shoulder, three tiny teeth in a mammoth rolling gear, stepped forty-five degrees left. Charlie tapped his marching cadence behind the line of men, their orderly steps taking on the precision of a Swiss watch.

A half mile forward, puffs of smoke made clear that Yankee artillery brought up from the rear had not been silenced by the rebel barrage. Hot shells trailed by white smoke arced across the sky, exploding overhead, sending shards of jagged iron slicing down on the advancing body of soldiers.

Men screamed, writhing on the grass; others fell without so much as a flinch, silently dead by the dozens. Other shells, twelve-pound solid balls of iron, struck the ground at angles that sent them bouncing head-on into the men, taking out a half dozen or more with each ball, heads severed, torsos torn from legs, legs and arms snapped like sticks.

Occasional dips in the terrain offered temporary, if imperfect, shelter, but such lulls were few and fleeting.

12

The men now met their most challenging field obstacle, second only to hot Union iron. Ahead, coursing diagonally across their path, lay the Emmitsburg Road, a major transportation artery leading to and from Gettysburg, each side of this road lined with stout rail fences. Already, elements of Longstreet's Corps had reached the fence but were unable to take it down. The fence would have to be scaled.

Union infantry, aware of this, at first stared in awe at the grand spectacle unfolding before them. Gathering their senses at the command of their officers, they waited eagerly patient, their rifles aimed straight, resting on a low stone wall, hammers at full cock, targets locked.

Shells ripped into the rebel ranks. Survivors gave an instinctive glance at the resulting horrors but maintained their steady, forward march.

Sterling's and Iverson's thinning line neared the first fence that bordered the road. Finster bolted forward, sensing the need to find the other side of its rails without pause and with all haste.

"Finster!" shouted Sterling.

"Clear the fence, boys!" he screamed as he tossed his rifle over its top and grabbed the top rail.

As he lifted his leg, a bullet slammed into his mouth, shattering his skull, sending blood and brain in all directions.

"My God!" Sterling whispered at the sight.

"Sure hope he settled things with Jesus," Henry whispered.

Charlie closed his eyes as he approached the fallen Finster and patted his drum harder.

Onward their lines marched.

"Sterling!" Charlie shouted.

Sterling turned at the sound of Charlie's voice.

"What is it, Charlie? We got to keep *movin*. Stay *low,* behind *me!"*

"Here," Charlie replied. "Take this."

"What?" Sterling asked in surprise. "Your *watch? Why?"*

"Take it, please. You're gon' need it! Trust me."

Sterling hadn't the time to argue. A shell exploded a few dozen feet to their front-right, bits of iron whistling past them, striking several soldiers. He took the watch from Charlie's hand and dropped it down his pants pocket.

"Thanks, Charlie. Now, let's *go!"*

13

Sterling and Iverson neared the Emmitsburg Road, which bisected the field parallel to their line of march. He slung his rifle over his shoulder and squeezed his way under the first of two fence's third rail. Henry Iverson followed closely behind. Bullets pecked and crunched into posts and scattered splinters of wood off rails and into soldiers' faces.

The enemy's aims were yet imperfect at this distance of four hundred yards, but on frightful occasion a bullet's path found a human target, especially those who stopped to offer assistance. A soldier, turning to yell a warning to Sterling, had his jaw taken off by a Minie ball. The soldier, blood and teeth and tongue oozing out the gaping hole, angry that he had been taken out of the fight so quickly, threw his rifle to the ground and began the trek back to his starting point. The severity of his wound also assured his removal from mortal existence, though his brain had not yet caught up to that certainty.

No one possessed the luxury of pondering fate's next move. Short of overt cowardice, forward, ironically, was the safest option for the unwounded.

Puffs of dirt spurted upwards from the road's soil. Men screamed as bullets punched holes into bellies and into legs an heads, into every conceivable point on the human body. In this mortal instant, lives once vibrant with energy, futures expectant with hope, were snuffed like candles from worldly existence.

Officers waved their swords, shouted their orders, exhorting their men to continue the charge. Men, with stoic compliance, obeyed, knowing that to turn and run was worse than anything coming at them now. Their duty in this moment required one of two outcomes: push the enemy off the ridge ahead or die trying. Anything less brought eternal shame upon the man and his family, and the soldiers took seriously this consequence.

The bent-yet-steady line of march from the Emmitsburg Road onward evolved quickly into chaotic irregularity, men staggered by the concussion of nearby shell explosions, others taking bullets and dropping. Flanking artillery fire from Little Round Top, a half mile to their right, destroyed rows of men, solid shot finding targets with relative ease. General Armistead ordered his lines to take an oblique-right alignment, facing their objective a hundred yards forward, a stand of trees on Cemetery Ridge, the very center of the Union line.

Sterling and Henry, along with a few thousand survivors, loaded their rifles as they marched, like machines performing methodic tasks, preparing for the climactic plunge, expecting at any second to feel the sting of death. Charlie continued his task of tapping his drum, unaware that such was any longer of minor consequence. The battle quickened into less of an organized assault and more of every man for himself.

Regiments from Pennsylvania, the 69th and 71st, defended the ground at the rebels' objective, that clump of trees. These men fired and loaded and fired again, with ceaseless fury and desperation, as rebel bullets clipped the Pennsylvanians' canteens and kepis and crushed flesh and bone. Unarmed standard bearers from both armies slammed dead to the earth, as their visible banners were considered valuable points of rally as well as invaluable spoils of war and thus viable military targets.

The guns of Lieutenant Alonzo Cushing's 4th U.S. Artillery Battery A kept up its terrible fire of canister, the balls ripping men apart and administering instant, painless obliteration.

A hundred feet from the Potomac Army's low stone wall, Sterling's rifle took two simultaneous bullets to its barrel, sending it flying in pieces from Sterling's hands. Shards of the barrel struck Sterling's left arm, chest, and shoulder, and he fell hard to the soil.

Sterling felt the wet warmth of his blood but could not feel any pain. No time to assess his wounds, he grabbed a dead soldier's rifle and struggled to regain his footing. He began the dutiful process of loading it. Spotting a Union infantryman aiming his rifle at the wounded Sterling, Charlie lunged between the infantryman and Sterling, just as the Yankee discharged his rifle.

"Charlie!" Sterling shouted.

The ball struck Charlie in his right side, spinning through his body and exiting his left side, sending the boy sprawling onto Sterling.

"Henry!" Sterling screamed amid the swirl of noise and chaos, blood and smoke, trying to get help to the wounded boy. *"Charlie's down!"*

Iverson swung his rifle like a club at the infantryman, smashing his skull, snapping the rifle.

"St … Sterling," Charlie managed, a surging weakness overwhelming his ability to speak. "Ain't … afraid to die. God's will …"

"Come fetch Charlie!" Sterling shouted. "He's *hit bad!* Get him out of here!"

"You're *both* hit!" Henry replied. "I'm coming!"

Iverson dropped his broken weapon and ran back to assist Sterling and Charlie, the latter of whom had passed. The remaining body of Confederates, in desperate need of support to secure their breach of the wall at the stand of trees, saw Iverson running rifle-less in a direction *away* from the crucible of battle, as if he were fleeing at the fight's most critical moment. In their minds, this was a Southern man's treasonous flight from the fight, not seeing the effort to assist two wounded comrades.

"Get *back* here, you *coward*!" some shouted, each tempted to turn his rifle on Iverson, believing he was running away when most needed.

At that instant, as Iverson reached Sterling and Charlie, Yankee bullets found their deadly marks, striking Henry's head, back, and both of his thighs. Sterling, unable to move and with Charlie's and Iverson's bodies atop his own, witnessed the takedown, knowing in this instant, more than at any other instant, the fight was hopeless, lost. He lay still, eyes closed, his hand pressed against his wounds, awaiting death or capture. He heard the inevitable outcome as the battle's final roar, the delirious cheers from the men of the Potomac Army's Second Corps, as the grand rebel charge melted into history.

14

Saturday evening, 8:13
July 4, 1863
Union field hospital
Home of Gettysburg resident, Lydia Leister

Unconscious, Sterling, along with other captured Confederate wounded, had been taken the previous day by Union ambulance corpsmen to a field hospital. There, he was given water and his wounds cleansed and bandaged. Dr. Digger McGuire attended his bedside, eager to discuss the battle from the perspective of an enemy combatant.

Sterling stirred from his sleep as McGuire sat on the bed. "What … where … where am I?"

"What's your name, soldier?"

"Vi … Sterling Vice."

"Who you with, Vice?"

"Who am I with?"

"Your unit, your regiment."

"Pickett's division, 38th Virginia, Armistead's brigade," Sterling answered, rubbing his bloodied shoulder. "I presume I am your captive?"

"You presume correctly."

"Still alive, thank God."

"Yes, but I wouldn't make any plans if I were you. You've lost a lot of blood."

The glint of McGuire's watch caught Sterling's eye. "What ... what day is it?" he asked, feeling the sharp pains in his shoulder and arm.

"Saturday," McGuire replied. "The fourth of July. A glorious day for our boys, our nation. Not so much for you and the rest of your ragged rebel bunch. Meade whipped you boys here, and I hear that Grant's taken Vicksburg. War's all but over."

"Where am I? Who are you?"

"Don't you remember? You were awake and thrashing yesterday evening. You even managed to write a letter, two, in fact. Don't worry, they'll be delivered … eventually.

"By the grace of God, you are in a Union hospital, being cared for by the best, though only God knows why. I am Doctor McGuire. Call me Digger."

"As in 'grave'?"

Doctor McGuire smiled. "As in bullet-remover."

"That … watch. Where'd you get it?"

"You like this watch, do you?" McGuire asked. "Aren't you in pain? I *hope* you are in pain. You do realize suffering is what soldiers do, don't you, especially rebel scum. I should take your blood, what's left of it, and give it to my own suffering lads, if only I had the means and the time. In my eyes, you have no rights here, no reason to ever again know comfort, and by all rights your blood is mine. But … I must follow my orders, for now. As for this watch … it *is* mine."

"I doubt that, sir!" Sterling said.

"How *dare* you dispute the word of a gentleman, a doctor, your *superior* and savior at that!"

"I know because you took that watch from *me*, out of *this* pocket," Sterling replied.

"I ... I did *no* such thing, you *lyin reb!*"

"Open it."

"*What*?"

"Open the watch. I can tell you what's inscribed on its face."

"Inscribed? Don't be ridiculous, man!"

"Open it. I will wager my life as a confessed spy, though I am not, to be shot if I cannot tell you its inscription," Sterling said. "But, if I am right, then you will agree to return the watch to me and promise I am paroled, along with *my* promise to never again take up arms against the United States of America."

"Don't you tell me--"

"*Do it*, doc!" a wounded Union soldier shouted. "But shoot him anyway! This rebel scum deserves to die!"

McGuire glanced toward the soldier and smiled. He opened the watch and read its inscription. He looked at Sterling and then in the direction of bedridden Union wounded. "Very well. I am a fair man. You've got yourself a deal, reb."

"It says, 'Joseph O. Neal, Neal spelled N-E-A-L. It's hand-painted in red. There is an etching of a sailing ship on the watch's back. Made by Columbia Watch Company, New York."

McGuire looked at the watch, turning it in his hand, and then turned to Sterling. "So it does, so it is. I must ask, how did you know this?"

"I know because the watch was in *my* pocket. That watch belongs -- belonged -- to a dear friend of mine, a twelve-year-old drummer boy killed by your men, one of these wounded perhaps," Sterling said as he scanned the beds filled mostly with Union wounded. "You've stolen it from me. How did *you* acquire that drum on the shelf?"

"The watch and drum were given to me by a private as thanks for treating his wound, a ball in his gut. Mortal, of course. No chance of survival, so he gave the watch and drum to me. Now it *belongs* to *me*, doesn't it. Spoils of war, you know. Amazing what turns up on a spent battlefield, even among rebel drummers. Doctors are demanded to do so much for so little in return. A bit of 'spoil' goes a long way, wouldn't you agree? Keeps us in this … horrible game."

McGuire snapped shut the watch's cover and returned it to his vest pocket.

"Now then, let me change your dressing. I'll grant you your freedom but not the watch. You'll be on your way come morning. No need to keep a rebel longer than necessary, consuming scarce resources he's not earned. Yes, you may leave on the morrow, if not sooner. A word of advice -- stay out of sharpshooter range. Of course, you can't, for obvious reasons. Lay back now, and let me assess your injuries."

Sterling rested his head against an improvised pillow, a rebel bedroll. Dr. McGuire peeled back Sterling's bloodied linens revealing a deep gash from his upper-left chest across his shoulder, as well as two other cuts deep into the flesh of his left-arm biceps, each of which revealed bone. The wounds issued a yellow-white pus and a reddening of color bordering the wounds' perimeters. Sterling winced with pain as the linens were removed.

"Hold still, now. Infection's setting in. But you've still got to leave tomorrow morning, wagers being as they are. You … might want to think about having that arm removed. I could render you that service."

Sterling saw across the room a Union soldier being prepped for the removal of his leg, chloroform being administered but slow to take effect. The soldier screamed and thrashed, requiring three others to hold him still.

"I'll pass, but thanks for your consideration."

"Where you from?"

"Does it matter?"

"To me, no, except for making conversation, but the farther you have to walk, the worse it will affect the healing of your wounds. Might be best to steer away from Lee's army. General Meade will either finish him here or catch up with him in a few days and finish the job. You might not want to be around when that happens." McGuire laughed. "Or, you could don the blue, heal your wounds here, eating decent food, and fight with Lincoln, for the Union and for the slaves. At least you would be on the right side of history. Of course, I would not expect you to betray your … country … and its slave-holding economy."

"I have family, children and a wife," Sterling said. "No slaves, nor would I ever think it right to own them."

"Then, why are you here, reb?"

"Because I witnessed your cavalry's total disregard for innocent life during one of their raids in a Southern town. I wasn't a soldier then, but I found my reason, then and there, to defend the new nation."

"A noble reason, perhaps," McGuire said. "I knew there had to be a worthy reason for bringing you into our fold. You are an honorable man. But it's too late in the war for magnanimity to matter much anymore. I should take your *good* arm now, legs, too, and give them to my boys. I've developed a procedure, first of its kind, for reattaching severed limbs. Wooden prosthetics will soon be a thing of the past. Perhaps I should give my procedure a real-world test right here? Of course, you'd be left limbless, but you just might become the first Confederate to receive the Medal of Honor for your sacrifice.

"On second thought, infection has likely spread throughout your body. You'd be no better than a Trojan horse, accomplishing here what you could not on the battlefield. Wouldn't want to risk spreading that infection."

Dr. McGuire applied fresh linens to Sterling's wounds and tended to the needs of other wounded. A nurse gave Vice a bowl of beef broth, a shot of whiskey, and some hardtack.

"Nurse?" Sterling said.

"Yes?"

"Could I ask a favor of you?"

"You may ask, of course. I can't promise I can do anything."

"Understood. Would you pen a letter for me, as I dictate?"

The nurse looked at Sterling and over to the departing McGuire. "I suppose I could. Keep it short, mind you."

"Short as I can, but I have more things that need sayin. Thank you."

"This might never make it to your family."

"And it won't if it's never written. I'm indebted to you, ma'am."

The nurse retrieved a quill pen, paper and ink. Sterling spoke the words slowly, measuring the value and economy of each. When she had finished, Sterling smiled and nodded his thanks. The nurse returned a smile, folded the letter and tucked it into her apron pocket. She later scribed a copy of the letter to keep in her safety until the war ended, her intentions to deliver it personally to ensure its eventual receipt.

15

Sunday morning, 6:36
July 5, 1863
Union field hospital, Leister house
Gettysburg, Pennsylvania

Next morning, Sterling, soaked in sweat, awakened, shouting, "*Miss Peasy*! Leave Miss Peasy *alone!* Henry was … a good …". Sterling's voice faded.

"Infection's much worse this morning, doctor," a nurse reported. "Fever of one-o-five, rising. If this keeps up, only place he's going today is to his grave."

"Looks as if he's already gone," McGuire observed. He separated the linen from the wound. "I thought I smelled it. Gangrene's set in. Leave him be."

"But, doctor, he'll … die."

"I said, *leave* him be. He'll die anyway. I'm not wasting more time and resources on an already-dead rebel. Suffering's what he *needs* now, with the time he has left. The more suffering he endures, the more likely the Lord will forgive his rebel ways and take him into His fold. Now, tend to someone else!"

The hours passed slowly. A nurse accompanied Doctor McGuire on his rounds that evening. McGuire noted the time on his newly-acquired pocket watch.

"9:53. Mister Vice still among us?"

"Yes, doctor," the nurse replied. "But almost gone."

"Looks like he's suffered enough. Hold my watch for me, please, whilst I fetch my bag. I'll give him some whiskey, to ease his pain."

Sterling's eyes opened wide. *"Leave her alone! Please*, sir, take me to Miss Peasy. Take me *now!* Take … me."

"Who is this Miss Peasy of whom he speaks?" asked McGuire as he left the room. "A brothel acquaintance, no doubt."

Ten minutes passed. Sterling's chest, rising and falling rapidly, heaved in a sudden burst, and he exhaled his last breath. The nurse placed her fingers over his nose. Feeling no movement of air, she lowered the sheet over his face and called for orderlies to remove the body.

"Time of death … 10:05," said the nurse, writing this in her notebook. "One last thing for you, Mr. Vice."

The nurse glanced toward the door. McGuire had not returned with the promised whiskey. She closed the lid on the watch and slid it deep into Sterling's pocket, an act which did not go unnoticed.

"Nurse!" shouted a wounded Union soldier. "What's that you put into that reb's pocket?"

"Nothing, sir, I was--"

"You were putting the watch back into his pocket, weren't you?"

"No, I--"

"Doctor McGuire!"

McGuire responded, thinking a soldier was in immediate distress.

"Nurse, tend to this man!" McGuire shouted.

"Doc, no, it's not that. She put your watch into that reb's pocket."

"What?"

McGuire grabbed the nurse's wrist with one hand and reached into Sterling's pocket with the other. He pulled the watch out, onto Sterling's cot.

"Sergeant, place this woman under arrest."

"Yes, sir."

"You are a *thief*, McGuire," she shouted.

"And *you* are a rebel sympathizer. Get her out of my sight."

The sergeant escorted the nurse to a holding facility.

Doctor McGuire turned facing Sterling's body. "So … you've died, have you?. As well you should. Take this man to the burial pit."

Orderlies lifted Sterling's body onto a stretcher. As they carried the body from the hospital tent, McGuire reached to retrieve the watch from Sterling's cot. As he did so, an incoming artillery shell, part of Lee's action to delay Union attacks while the main body of Confederate forces escaped westward, burst above the tent. Shrapnel tore through the tent, a few pieces striking McGuire, killing him.

After an hour of frenzied efforts to remove wounded to another facility farther to the rear, the damaged hospital was abandoned. The watch lay unnoticed on the ground, under a blanket.

16

Sterling Vice ambled the lonely country roads as he stared at vaguely familiar landmarks. Mister Palmer's barn, Sterling noted, seemed quite older, its paint all but peeled away and its boards grayed.

Not like old man Palmer to leave holes in his roof unpatched, thought Sterling. *War damage, no doubt.*

"Avery's farm is … *gone?*" Sterling said, shocked, no one near to hear his discovery. "And what the devil is … *that?*"

Approaching Sterling over a ridge ahead came a hard-galloping horse, its rider urging the stallion onward with side-to-side thrashings of his crop. The rider brought the horse to a turf-tearing stop near Sterling.

"Sterling Vice?" the rider asked.

"That I am, sir. And who—"

"Take this," the rider said, extending his clenched, gloved fist. Spreading his fingers, he dropped a cloth-covered object into Sterling's palm. "Keep it with you. Never surrender it."

"What is it?" Sterling asked, looking at the object, peeling back the cloth. "A *watch?*" He opened it. "*The* watch! *Charlie's* watch."

"You are to go into Raventon and seek Miss Peasy Parlevous."

"Miss Peasy—"

"When you find her, you will then know what you are to do next.

"But beware," said the rider. "There is another who seeks this watch, one whom you know, one who embodies evil and has committed such undetected evil in Raventon for years. His time for repentance draws to a close, after which he will spend his eternity in hell, *unless* he can take this watch from you. If he does so, his time of existence in this realm will be prolonged, his acts of evil continued.

"Beware of false prophets, which come to you in sheep's clothing, but inwardly they are ravening wolves.

"You have a mission and a short while to fulfill that mission, after which you will join your blessed loved ones and Jesus once again. But if the evil one takes possession of this watch, his work will continue. Seek out Miss Peasy Parlevous."

Confused beyond measure, Sterling's mind issued glimpses of his having heard of Miss Peasy Parlevous. He could not discern any connection. Sterling looked up from the watch to ask the rider about the watch's powers, why a mere watch, an inanimate object, had been given such powers.

But the rider was gone. Not a trace of his being there, except for the echoes of his words … and this watch.

Sterling pocketed the watch and continued his walk, pausing to assess things familiar and things beyond his comprehension, unsure of when and how he had arrived home and less sure of what had transpired during those hundreds of miles between

Gettysburg and Raventon. The air felt warmer, stickier. Leaves and field grass waved in the breeze like green oceans. All that was certain was that his shoulder had healed somewhere along the way, his left arm still in a sling.

Home had changed, in ways unexpected.

Wars ... and time ... do that.

17

Friday morning, 11:37
July 4, 2020
Home of Miss Peasy Parlevous

Miss Peasy issued a low groan as she pressed her hands down on the arms of her wicker chair. The relative cool of the morning began its transition into the blast of merciless eastern summer sunrays. Slowly, she maneuvered her body to a standing position, a grinning wince of defiance toward the stream of pain coming from all regions of her elderly form. She gave a celebratory sigh of thanks at this small, significant affirmation that life still coursed through her veins. She counted her victories these days as anything that kept her cognizant, upright, and breathing. Age had taken its toll, even on the stubborn Miss Peasy Parlevous, yet she offered only smiles and gratitude for a life well-lived.

Miss Peasy had ceased her flying days two years ago, selling her beloved Cessna, Flossy. Occasionally, Flossy's new owner flew low over the neighborhood's trees and houses, specifically Miss Peasy's trees and house, and gave a gentle acknowledging tip of the plane's wings as it roared overhead. Flossy was a welcomed sight to her tired eyes and to the ensconced routine of an era passed. But even those flyovers had diminished as the months passed.

Smoking her briarwood pipes, on the other hand, remained entrenched in her daily routine. She had relented, with her typical stubbornness, to the nagging grip of truth that no longer whispered, but *shouted*, telling indeed in the clearest of terms that even *her* days, her routines, were numbered. Still, her smoldering pipes remained immortal, and she would not surrender the habit until life surrendered her.

Acknowledging the inevitable drainage of time, she had summoned the help of neighbors to retrieve from her attic such trunks filled with ancestral memorabilia and personal artifacts of her own memories. Revisiting these relics and memories were now her priority, her race against life's relentless clock and an ever-closer finish line.

Pressing her palm upon her cane, marking her measured steps on creaking 200-year-old oakwood planks, she made her way to a waiting tray of steaming Earl Grey tea and a creamer of imported two-percent goat's milk. She lowered her stiff body to the sofa, and grasping a pipe filled with the dying embers of Virginia flake-cut, she puffed it back to life.

"Ah, yes," she whispered, exhaling, her tired eyes wincing as the smoke curled toward her face. "Kept me alive for goin on a century. Never too old for this."

Nor was she too old to make and consume her blue-ribbon apple pies, as she cut a warm bite with a fork. Returning the pipe to its smolder, she lifted her platinum creamer with a gentle shake in her grip, and tipped it, allowing a measured stream of the two-percent into her cup of tea. She stirred the liquids together and took the cup into the careful hold of her fingers, bringing it to her lips. She sipped.

"Ahhh." She smiled, taking another sip, followed by the bite of pie. "It's the simple things."

She took the key from the tea tray and turned her eyes to the wooden box at her feet.

"Now, then," she wondered aloud with heightened expectations, "what might be awaiting my discovery in this box?"

After all, this box had not been opened, these treasures not examined, since before they were given to her by her mother some fifty-three years earlier, passed down to her all but unnoticed in their generational flow.

She inserted and turned the key and lifted the box's cherry lid. Earthy, rustic odors of arid wood and the spirits of imprisoned years drifted into her nostrils. Not knowing where to start, not that a certain starting point mattered, she inhaled slowly, as if absorbing all those years once again. She fingered randomly through the box's contents of yellowed letters, diaries, tattered Bible testaments, embroidered handkerchiefs, and other relics passed on from Civil War ancestors and those who followed.

As if whispered in her ear, she stopped her roaming fingers on a random grouping of documents and pulled out a letter from among scores of dormant correspondences.

The face of the letter's envelope was adorned with the magnificent curves and curls of the lettering of nineteenth-century penmanship, lightly legible now, but legible nonetheless. Its unpretentious address read:

Miss Elizabeth Vice
Wedowee, Alabama

She lifted the yellowed parchment, stiff and dry with age, from its envelope, careful not to pull on the paper's creases.

"June 30, 1863," she whispered.

Miss Peasy pushed her spectacles to the bridge of her nose and through the slight blur read slowly,

whispering each word's careful annunciation, adjusting upward the glasses' downward slide every few words.

"'Tuesday, June 30, 1863
"'My Dearest Elizabeth,

"'Hope these words find you well. Don't know when I might be able to write you again, and whilst things are a bit quiet, I will take the opportunity here to write you a few lines.

"'I am enjoying the rarity of hot coffee, salt pork, and cakes of corn, a small ration the army was able to secure from the town we now occupy. We are in Pennsylvania, truly a land of plenty. The corn is tall and everywhere. The soldiers laugh and sing and chase after pigs and chickens like children after butterflies. The army is eating as we have not been able to in a long while.

"'I fought in my first battle on the evening of 2 May, near a crossroads community of Chancellorsville (Virginia), and I must tell you that I want no part of any battle ever again. I was shot, but by the grace of God I was saved by, of all things, a Bible given me by a fellow soldier, the pages of which absorbed the bullet's energy, stopping the bullet's point at Isaiah 48:9. Look up the verse. You will be just as amazed as I. I do not know what became of the soldier who gave this Bible to me, wounded as he was in his belly, but I was blessed by its receipt. I enclose that Bible for you as a symbol of God's mercy and to secure in your hands for posterity.

"'If the snap of a finger could take me to your side, my beloved Elizabeth, I would be there now. There is nothing glorious about battle, nothing at all, rest assured. It is nothing more than horrific bloodletting and suffering, misery on a scale unimaginable until seen and experienced. Battles are ferocious, desperate affairs.

Bullets and shells whistle and scream all around, and the prospect of being hit leaves a man with an intolerable anxiety, manageable only in the context and immediacy of the demands and distractions of battle. O, the horrible sounds of screams and groans of men shot in every conceivable point on their bodies, men clinging to life far from home, far from loved ones, all out of pure force of will and love of family! There are no 'nice' wounds, no 'good' wounds. But, alas, there is more.

"'Word is we are on the cusp of another great battle, which will be my second great battle in as many months, the first being in the fields and forests surrounding a tiny crossroads somewhere in Virginia, Chancellorsville, as I previously noted.

"'My regiment, part of division commander, George Pickett's, A.P. Hill's corps, Army of Northern Virginia, is being held in reserve in Chambersburg, Pennsylvania, west of the main body of

Lee's army, now located some fifteen miles east of us, near Cashtown. I have just been ordered to report to General Longstreet's First Corps, McClaw's brigade, which means another march of fifteen miles.

"'Don't know a whole lot more to share with you. We have been on pressed marches since the days after Chancellorsville, moving northward, I presume, to take this war to Yankee soil. Virginia, indeed, is a devastated landscape and is in need of a healing, as is all of our country and all of her people.

"'I do not know where the Yankees are in relation to our army, nor is it my business to know, but I can only presume they are moving northward as well, paralleling us, which foretells another clash of arms. Word is that elements of their cavalry have been spotted on our right flank, keeping us in their sights and shielding us from discovering their main body. I fear, my dear Elizabeth, that this next clash of arms may be my last, premonitions being so much a part of that inexplicable fog of war.

"'Keep me in your prayers, as you are in mine. I love you. Be sure to tell the children I love them.

"'As always,

"'Your devoted Sterling

"'P.S. Do you hear from Henry Iverson?'"

"Sterling Vice," Miss Peasy whispered. "The husband of a close friend of my great-great grandmama's. That'd be Elizabeth Vice. The battle he alludes to can only be Gettysburg. Henry Iverson, one of my great-great grandmama's sons, bless his soul, has been the *bane* of my existence, my family's existence, for all these years since."

Miss Peasy shook her head and sifted through other documents in the box, checking for dates and visible postmarks, hoping to discover from dates on envelopes any follow-up letters. None was found. She also rifled through the box's contents in search of the bullet-shot Bible. Perhaps, Miss Peasy reckoned, Sterling's premonition came true.

"Ah," she said in astonished satisfaction. "*The Bible!*"

She pulled it out from its frame of papers and memorabilia. Indeed, a hole had penetrated its cover, the distorted crusty-gray bullet still firm within the pages, the Word.

"I must ask Taylor's help in researching this Sterling Vice and his service in Lee's Army of Northern Virginia, as well as Mr. Vice's fate. Maybe some letters in this box will give some clues."

Miss Peasy took her pipe, drawing again on its smolder, resurrecting its burn, reliving, if briefly, the eloquence, the timelessness, of its aged flavor. She smiled, reaching for her Earl Grey.

18

July 4, 2020
Whippoorwill Diner
Raventon, GA
6:35 PM

The Whippoorwill was abuzz, the evening crowd enjoying its standard fare of Southern cooking. Taylor Smart called it "Southern fattening", but a team of horses could not pull her away from the tastes and temptations it offered.

She entered the diner, her eyes darting left and right in anticipation of seeing friends she had not seen in over a year. She sported her gold-and-green William and Mary tee-shirt and shoulder-length brown hair. She had grown a couple of inches since the summer of '19, late spurts she had not seen coming but welcomed nonetheless.

Extra growth notwithstanding, she stood on her tiptoes looking for Bobbie Leigh and Rommy. Why he had opted for the altered name of Rommy, a moniker derived from his middle name of Romulus, versus his given first name of Pilfree, baffled her. Though, upon reflection, the name did sound a bit more collegiate and less cartoonish than did 'Pilfree'.

After all, Pilfree Romulus Bojo – Rommy – was now president of his rising sophomore class at Harvard, not to mention riding the crest of a full scholarship. His sights, Taylor last heard, were set on law and politics.

As for Bobbie Leigh, Taylor was anxious to learn more about what she'd been up to. Knowing Bobbie Leigh, no obstacle in her way stood a snowball's chance.

Craning her neck, Taylor heard a shout.

"Taylor! *Taylor Smart!*"

That voice, that *unmistakable* voice!

Then she saw the wave of a hand above the sea of humans waiting in line to either pay their bills or to be seated.

Bobbie Leigh pushed her way through the crowd, to the front of Taylor. Her long, blue hair, as straight and silky-smooth as an ascot, cascaded off her scalp and shoulders like a mountain stream.

In unison, each shouted the other's name and wrapped arms around each other.

"It's so *good* to see you, Bobbie Leigh," Taylor said through her glistening smile. "You don't look a day over twenty!"

"Flattery will get you *everywhere,*" she replied. "And It's *Bobbie*. I've dropped the Leigh part."

"You *have*, haven't you! Rommy mentioned that, but I didn't know if he was kidding. Well then … *Bobbie* … you're as gorgeous as ever."

"Don't I *know* it!" Both laughed.

"Where's Pil … I mean Rommy?" Taylor shook her head. "That's going to take some getting used to, probably more so than the name Pilfree itself."

"He even looks more Rommy-ish than Pilfree. Not nearly the doofus he was four years ago. Kind of cute, actually," Bobbie said with a wink and a mischievous grin.

"Oh *really?*" Taylor replied, looking ahead around swarms of faces. "So, where is this new persona?"

"Back there. Follow me." Bobbie took Taylor's hand and pulled her through the crowd. "One thing hasn't changed; he's still a full-blown nerd."

"Good to know," Taylor replied with a smile. "I like tradition."

Taylor and Bobbie approached the booth occupied by Rommy, his back facing them. Taylor crept up behind him and placed her hands over his eyes.

"Three guesses! First two don't count!"

"Uhh … Melania Trump! No, that can't be right. Ummm … Golda Meir!"

"Golda Meir?" Taylor and Bobbie said, a cringed scrunch on their faces.

"You said the first two didn't count," Rommy said, turning. "Well, well, Who are *you?*"

"Hey there, you ol' *scalawag*," Taylor said, hugging Rommy. "Let me look at you."

"Don't look too closely," Bobbie noted. "In fact, step back. And squint."

"Navy jacket; bowtie; crisp, white shirt; khakis. What's Harvard *done* to you, Mr. *President?*" Taylor asked, holding back her laughter and brushing a few specks of dandruff from his lapel. "What, *no checkered tennis shoes?*"

"That's Mr. *Class* President," Rommy replied. "Same ol' doofus; just different packaging."

"More like *classless* Class President," Bobbie said.

"All right, you. Wow, it is so good to see you, Taylor." Rommy looked Taylor over, head to toe. "Princeton has definitely been good to *you*, girl."

"Careful," Bobbie warned.

Someone deposited some coins into the corner jukebox. Oldies night at the Whippoorwill Diner, specifically a Rosemary Clooney oldie.

"You make me feel so young;
you make me feel there are songs to be sung,
bells to be rung,
and a wonderful fling to be flung ..."

"I *love* this song," Taylor said.

"*Love* it? How do you even *know* it?" Bobbie said.

"I have old parents, remember? And, Rommy, I can't complain, can't complain at all. What's Harvard like?"

"Just like Princeton - old, snobby and *way* too liberal."

"Found your safe-space yet?"

"Ha! Lawyers *are* safe-spaces."

The three laughed and took their seats. Rommy motioned over a server.

"So, you're a Pre-law major," Taylor said.

"Yeah, I guess."

"You're not sure?"

"All depends on how my contract law class goes. So far, so good, but my instructor is very much like John Houseman's character in the 70s show, 'Paper Chase'. Relentlessly demanding and not the slightest hint of a sense of humor. One can feel the crushing weight of the expectation of perfection."

"And law is nothing if not imperfect," Taylor observed.

"Sometimes the reasoning behind the law is a bit suspect," Rommy admitted, "and its interpretations have become more an art form involving persuasion over the letter. That's where the perfection comes in."

"More like muddled and befuddled, you mean," Bobbie said.

"Seems I recall you were pretty good at delivering perfection," Taylor observed. "Never forget, my dear Rommy, that you've already passed a very stringent, real-world contract-law class from having played Blythington's game."

"Don't remind us. What a lesson in contracts *that* was!" Bobbie added.

"Indeed," Rommy said. "Got another real-world challenge coming up second semester next year."

"What's that?" asked Taylor.

"A couple of us have offered some pro bono assistance to a legal team out in California, Humboldt

County, someplace called Alderpoint. Investigations of missing persons, even murder. They need some 'go-fers', and it's a great opportunity to conduct some genuine field work and maybe earn a feather or two for my resume. Marijuana capital of America, you know."

"Oh, yeah, there's that," Bobbie said sarcastically after a gasp of surprise, "Dear God, Rommy, *don't* get yourself involved in that sort of thing!"

"We'll be safe, Bobbie, don't worry. Ours is a behind-the-scenes involvement, really more desk work than field work."

"You *do* know what they call that place, that Alderpoint place, don't you?" Taylor asked.

Rommy hesitated to answer, but he knew the answer.

"So ... other than its name, Alderpoint, what *do* they call it?" Bobbie asked. Rommy looked at Taylor.

"You brought it up," Taylor said.

"I did, didn't I." Rommy sighed. "Murder Mountain," he muttered, clearing his throat, head down as if to muffle his words.

"*What* mountain?" Bobbie asked, startled. I'm going to pretend I did *not* hear that, Pilfree!"

"Ah, so *that's* what it takes to restore order," Taylor said, smiling.

"By the way, Taylor, how *is* Uncle Blythington?" Rommy smiled.

"Content," she answered.

"Y'all ready t' order, honey?" the server asked robotically, smacking her chewing gum as she pulled the order pad from her apron pocket.

"I do believe we are," Rommy said, bent over his menu. "They still got our usuals, if you're game."

"Sounds great to me," said Taylor, "but I think I'll broaden my horizons a bit. Chicken Marsala, please, and water to drink."

"Since when did the Whippoorwill go Italian?" Bobbie asked, closing the menu. "I'll have the same, I guess."

"Forget the usuals. Make it three marsalas," chimed Rommy. "One check, please."

"Why, *thank you*, kind sir!" Taylor said.

"And give it to *her*," Rommy instructed, pointing to Bobbie.

"What?"

"Kidding, Bobbie. Give it to me."

The server rolled her eyes, gathered the menus and jotted a few notes on her order pad as she walked away.

"So, Bobbie, what's new with you?" Taylor asked.

"Haven't you heard, Taylor?" Rommy asked.

"Apparently *not*, Rommy," she answered.

"Heard what, Bobbie?"

19

"Oh, nothing, really," she answered.

"Nothing!" Rommy said, feigning frustration. "You *cut* me to my core! I should say it's quite *something.*"

Taylor smiled, fingers tapping the table top, awaiting one of them to reveal the news. "Okay, so …"

"Bobbie's got herself a boyfriend," Rommy said.

"Okay, and …" Taylor replied, thinking there had to be more, a name perhaps. "Anyone I know?"

"Likely," Rommy said. Bobbie smiled.

"Then *who?"* Taylor asked.

"You're *looking* at him," Rommy said.

"Seriously? You, Rommy? *You're* Bobbie Leigh's *boyfriend?"*

"The very same," Rommy replied.

"And it's *Bobbie*, Taylor."

"Yes, I know, but you sort of caught me off guard. I mean, Bobbie, for the love of *Pete*, our Pilfree … *Rommy* … was your *doofus,* and not *that* many years ago. What *happened?*"

"Let's keep Pete out of this," Rommy chimed.

"Just grew up, I guess," Bobbie said, shrugging.

"Got *that* right," Rommy echoed.

"Well, then," Taylor said, clearing her throat as she processed the news, "are we still spending the break together?"

"Absolutely," Bobbie said, "and I have this feeling it's going to be a *doozy* of a break."

20

"So, how are *we* spending this break, now that I know you two are an item?" Taylor asked. "Can't want a third wheel hanging around you."

"Not spending it like *that* guy, I hope," Rommy replied, tilting his head in the direction of a booth ahead and to his left.

The girls turned their heads slowly, slyly, as if observing faulty ceiling lighting, not wanting to expose their obvious intentions. In that booth sat an old man, a black, broad-brimmed Amish hat upon his head, tangled white frizz streaming down shoulder-length. The man hunched over his bowl of soup and bread, protecting it like a wolf. He held a spoon to his lips, slurping its contents. His ebony eyebrows –

rather, one continuous brow, individual hairs zig-zagging like wilderness vines - seemed to crawl horizontally, as would a caterpillar over stony ground. Below his eyes were two hanging sacks of skin, purpled and wrinkled, holding within them all the sleepless years of his age, all the weight of his experiences.

The man lifted a spoonful of soup toward his mouth, droplets falling to his lap as he tilted to pick something from his vest pocket. Finding nothing to pick, he glanced up from his spoon, his steel-gray eyes catching the three in their gaze. Embarrassed, the three turned away.

"Wow, he's a tad spooky, wouldn't you say?" Bobbie whispered.

"Doesn't look like *his* weekend, any of his days, for that matter, are the sorts of doozies one brags about," Taylor said.

"I know," agreed Rommy. "Think we ought to pay for his meal?"

"I think that's a *great* idea, sweetie." Bobbie said.

"Oh, *way* not used to this!" Taylor said, shaking her head. You *do* realize you just called your favorite doofus 'sweetie'."

"Realize it, and proud to do it," Bobbie said, smiling, as she gave Rommy a kiss on the ear.

"I'll ask the server to give us his ticket," Rommy said.

"May not appreciate charity, Rommy," Taylor warned.

"And you would be correct, young lady," the old man said, standing bent by their table, the carved wood of a skull-capped cane in one hand and a smudged, leather-covered Bible in the other. An antique military drum was slung across his shoulder, tapping people as they tried to walk by the narrow passage between him and a row of customers' booths. Drops of soup meandered through his beard, one drop plopping upon the cover of his Bible. He raised the Bible to his lips and licked the drop of soup.

Startled, the three lurched back.

"When did you … *how* did you …," Rommy struggled to ask.

"Time is of the *essence!* You kids are no different from the rest," the man replied as he reached again for his vest pocket, as if to grab hold of something, perhaps a pocket watch or a pen. He slapped the vest pocket a few times before realizing the pocket was empty. "Caught up in *yourselves* and your blasted *smartphones.* Not the *least* bit willing to sacrifice, to *really* sacrifice, to lay down your *lives,* your *blood,* for others. You assuage your sense of guilt by … what do you call it … paying it forward. Hmmph! 'Twas *easy* making my way to your table unnoticed. Could have cut off your heads before you knew what was happening, so wrapped up in yourselves, you are. I'll just be paying for my *own* meals. I have *real* currency, not that worthless Confederate paper you people use. Go on back to your self-indulgences. But remember, 'Vengeance is mine, sayeth the Lord'."

The old man turned and hobbled toward the cash register, repeatedly taking his hand to his empty vest pocket, as if by instinct, the drum alternately slapping his left side and the shoulders of customers with near-perfect cadence.

"Okay," Taylor said, sliding her smartphone into her pocket. "Did *not* see that coming."

"Not to mention that old relic of a drum," Bobbie added. "What's up with *that*!"

"Whew. Let me catch my breath," Rommy said. "Old man could use a bath or six. Isn't that Travis McGuire, former preacher from Cornerstone Covenant Church? *Crazy* Travie."

"Very same," Taylor answered. "Caught up in some malfeasance several years ago, involving his secretary and some collection plates. They say he bought that Civil War drum, a Confederate drum, with church tithes. Paid thousands of dollars, allegedly. That sort of explains his reference to Confederate currency, maybe."

"Now *there's* a story," Bobbie said.

"He denies having anything to do with his secretary," Taylor continued, "and he claims the money was owed him for back-pay and lost vacation time. Bought that old Civil War drum with it, they say. Others say he's *always* had that drum. Who knows what or who to believe. Rather than the church taking legal action, they fired him instead."

"Isn't he the sort of client you'd like to defend, Rommy?" Bobbie asked.

"Depends on whose print of currency he uses for payment."

"Crazy Travie still says he was 'unjustly terminated'," Taylor continued, "and that nobody so much as lifted a finger to his defense, saying - and I quote - 'as in the old days'. He preaches on street corners these days, relying on the kindness of strangers. A pretty lonely individual, if you ask me."

"I hear he puts on a show at those street corners, he and that old drum," Bobbie said. "Uses that drum to draw attention, as if he needed *any* prop to accomplish that."

"Preaches personal sacrifice," Taylor added. "Says suffering is good, that it's a major part of God's plan of salvation for each of us, that it teaches us gratitude and perspective and compassion for others, and that we *deserve* all the suffering we get, not so much as punishment but for the value of the lessons learned. But we can't suffer, says he, without sacrifice, as Christ suffered on the Cross. Thus, according to Preacher McGuire, sacrifice begets suffering begets salvation. No suffering, no salvation."

"Sounds like a maker of great conversation," Rommy said wryly, taking a sip of water.

"If by 'great' you mean *wacky*, and by 'conversation' you mean *babble*," Bobbie said.

"They don't call him Crazy Travie for nothing."

"I think he's little more than a harmless eccentric," Taylor said as she watched him exit the diner, "nothing to worry about. But I'll give him one thing."

"Here you go, kids," said the server, balancing three plates of chicken marsala on the length of her left arm and a tray of three glasses of water in her right hand. "Do me a favor, honey, and take this tray of waters," the server said to Rommy.

Bobbie smiled and winked at Rommy.

Rommy took the tray and distributed the glasses, spilling nary a drop. The server deftly set each plate of chicken marsala in front of each of the three.

"Look all right?" she asked.

"Looks great," they replied together, sniffing the wafting aromas.

"Enjoy. Chicken marsala is my favorite. I'll check back in a few."

"So, what one thing will you *'give him'*, Taylor," Bobbie asked, twirling pasta and mushrooms with her fork.

"Well, Preacher McGuire may be a few minutes short of an hour, but he *was* a staunch defender of Miss Peasy back in the days when she was being mercilessly derided by Raventon townsfolk as the 'Witch of Raventon'."

"*Defended* her?" Rommy asked. "How so?"

"During one of my visits with her back shortly after we moved to Raventon – you know how she loves her Earl Grey tea and smoking her pipe –"

"And sitting in her wicker chairs," Rommy added.

"Loves making apple pies and eating her Zippy burgers, too," Bobbie said. They laughed.

"Yes, Zippies, too," Taylor said, her mind's eye glancing away to a time not so many years ago. "And how she *loved* flying Flossy! Anyway, Miss Peasy confided in me all the bullying and ridicule she had received from some Reventonians. All of her life, she said."

"Bullying?"

"Yes, and that's putting it mildly. Miss Peasy's local heritage goes all the way back to the Revolutionary War years. During the Civil War, her great-great grandmother, Rebecca Iverson, had a son, Henry, who was a friend of Sterling Vice's."

"Wait a minute, Taylor," Bobbie interrupted. "You're throwing names at us like confetti on a parade. Who's Rebecca Iverson, did you say, and her son, Henry, and Sterling Vice? I *do* like that name, though, Sterling. Rolls off the tongue."

"Not *bad*, Bobbie," Taylor said, smiling. "You threw that confetti right back, not missing a piece! Sterling Vice, so I'm told, besides being Henry

Iverson's friend, was also sort of a Raventon hero, having taken a bullet to his shoulder during a Yankee cavalry raid in Raventon back in early winter of 1863."

"*Sort* of?" said Rommy. "The man's got his on *statue* inside City Hall. Raventon adores him."

"Man, I have *got* to get down to City Hall more often," Bobbie said.

"So, what's all this have to do with Miss Peasy's Witch of Raventon moniker?" Rommy asked.

"Getting to that," Taylor replied. "The way I heard the story, Sterling was shot in the right shoulder during that raid while shielding a twelve-year-old orphan boy from a saber-slashing horseman.

"Local lore says that Vice and that twelve-year-old boy marched off together to join Lee's army in spring of 1863 and that - and here's the part that points to Miss Peasy's bullying - Henry, having joined the army a couple of years earlier than Sterling, was, well ... shot in the back running away from the fighting at Gettysburg. Through the generations, Miss Peasy's family, and now Miss Peasy herself, have borne the brunt of local derision, tormented for Henry's alleged cowardice, though, obviously, such was no fault of hers.

"As you might know, cowardice during the days of the Civil War was worse than death itself. Showing the white feather, as it was sometimes referred to, was something that never sat well with the soldiers, the veterans, even contemporary diehard Southern historians and locals well after that war. Just part of our Southern tradition that still lives."

"What, for getting *shot*?" Bobbie asked. "I thought that sort of thing made one a *hero*."

"In the *back*," Rommy said, "and *running away*. Not exactly the stuff of heroes."

"What became of Sterling Vice?" asked Bobbie.

"Missing in action and presumed dead. Never came home."

"One more thing that underscores how serious this has been for Miss Peasy, all her life. Her daddy was *lynched* because of this, back in 1934. Miss Peasy was twelve years old then."

"Lynched?"

"Taken from his bedroom at midnight. Tied to a tree, whipped with a cat-o-nine tails, and left to rot in the July-Georgia sun," Taylor said. "Made Miss Peasy watch."

"But why *lynched?*" Rommy asked.

"Miss Peasy didn't say, but she made it pretty clear Southerners for decades took Lee's loss at Gettysburg hard. They never blamed Lee himself for the errors made at Gettysburg. Instead, for many years, they blamed General James Longstreet, Lee's 'Old War Horse' and top field commander after Stonewall Jackson died, saying he was the reluctant warrior during that battle, never agreeing that the Army of Northern Virginia should have sought to fight an offensive battle on northern soil. Longstreet preferred that Lee stay on the *defensive*, as he had done at Sharpsburg the previous September, the strategy being to wear down the North's will to fight.

"Any news telling of a local having turned and run from a fight, especially at Gettysburg, only reinforced the hatred some Southerners came to feel for Longsteet."

"Why such anger directed at this Longstreet fellow?" Bobbie asked.

"Long story, Bobbie," Taylor replied, "but the short version is that Longstreet lacked any enthusiasm in carrying out Lee's orders of battle on the second and third days at Gettysburg. Longstreet preferred -- and argued for on day two of the battle -- flanking the Union army, getting behind that army and forcing General Meade to attack Lee, rather than Lee attacking Meade head-on. He delayed the ordered attack, Pickett's Charge, even argued with Lee about the wisdom of it, until well into the afternoon. Then he opted not to send in any meaningful support when it became obvious the attack was faltering. A handful of Pickett's men breached the stone wall at the Angle but saw no units of support coming. The attack ended with over six thousand Confederate casualties in a span of half an hour. Longstreet got the blame, as did anyone caught in the ultimate act of Southern shame -- cowardice.

"Back home, they took their anger out on those they could *reach*, the locals, such as the Iverson family and all of those who followed.

"Anyway, folks labeled Miss Peasy as the Witch of Raventon for "spells" she allegedly cast upon those relentless tormentors, some of whom disappeared quite *mysteriously* in the years following. Some, I'm told, were found, their bodies mutilated, limbs and organs missing, drained of their blood. Gruesome stuff, if true."

"Wow. Gruesome, indeed," Rommy said. "Was Miss Peasy ever *charged* with these crimes?"

"Harassed, yes. Accused, yes. Laughed at, yes. Charged, no. Insufficient evidence, obviously. But the court of public opinion certainly charged her. Found her guilty as well, unfortunately. She's been serving a life sentence ever since."

"So, how did Preacher McGuire defend her?" Rommy asked.

"He believed she had suffered enough for events beyond her control. Unfortunately, Crazy Travie and his 'wacky babble' defending the Witch of Raventon was akin to a heart attack defending arteriosclerosis. It was all rather pointless and did her more harm than good."

"Say *what?*" Bobbie said. "I lost you after 'wacky babble'."

"Who was the orphan boy?" Rommy asked.

"Interesting you should ask," Taylor replied, taking a bite of chicken and pasta. "Miss Peasy tells me the boy was inserted as a *drummer* into General George Pickett's division of Virginians, serving with Sterling and Henry at Gettysburg."

"So?" Bobbie asked.

Taylor and Rommy stared at Bobbie, waiting for the dots to be connected.

"Ohhh!" Bobbie said, dropping a forkful of marsala onto her plate.

"Makes that *drum* of *Crazy Travie's* all the creepier," Rommy said.

21

"So, fittingly stuffed, what shall we do tonight?" Rommy asked as he leaned back and draped his right arm around Bobbie's shoulders.

"There's always Raventon's spectacular fireworks show," Bobbie said. *"Not!"*

"Anything that doesn't require a lawyer," Taylor said, grinning. "Make that, anything that doesn't require the *services* of a lawyer. We'll take the lawyer-in-the-rough we have now."

"Are you saying the lawyer we know is better than the lawyer we *don't* know?" Bobbie asked.

"Something like that," Taylor replied, laughing.

Dessert was enjoyed over small talk and the challenges facing second-year college students.

"Let's take a spin downtown. Haven't paid much attention to it for quite a while now, but I hear it has changed," Taylor said.

"Beats bowling, I guess," Bobbie said.

"I'd like to take a look at that new music shop," Taylor said. "Music and More is it?"

"They sell *instruments,* Tay," Bobbie noted, "not CDs or vinyls."

"Duly noted, Bobbie, but I'm … strangely interested in guitars, acoustic guitars, the six-string variety, tiger maple and aspen, Martins, if they have 'em."

"What's got into you, girl," Bobbie asked, smiling. "I didn't know you had developed this musical interest of playing. And speaking of arms and legs, Martins aren't cheap, you know."

"Always had that interest. My roommate has one. She lets me play it. My interest in owning one just never seemed so strong until … well, *now.*" Taylor smiled, as if apologizing in advance for this sudden quirk. "And I don't want to learn just *any* songs. Specific tunes, Civil War tunes, the ones the soldiers loved."

"First, Mr. Wacky Babble. Now *you're* scaring me, Tay," Bobbie said.

"I think it's cool, Bobbie," said Rommy. "Let's take a ride down to Music and More and check out their selections of guitars. It'll be fun."

"Oh, I'm game, sweetie. Just have never seen this side of Taylor. What specific Civil War songs?"

"Camp songs, marching songs, the ones the regimental bands would play, to perk up the men's morale, to keep them fighting-focused, not death-focused. Maybe it's all this talk of Civil War stuff."

"Maybe we'll run into Crazy Travster along the way," Bobbie said.

"Crazy *Travie,*" Rommy corrected.

"The man never met a street corner he did not like," Taylor said. "Draws crowds like a circus sideshow."

"Hmmm," Bobbie said, "let's go find us a sideshow."

"Sounds good. Beats bowling," Taylor said with a wink.

"Okay, but what about Music and More?" Rommy asked.

"Sideshow first," Taylor replied. "My investigative radar is flashing."

"Sounds like a job for the Raventon Three," Bobbie said. "Going to be an *interesting* night."

22

"Whoa, *he* looks lost," Rommy observed, looking out the booth window as they were readying to leave the Whippoorwill. Rommy checked the tab and placed forty-five dollars under a glass of water.

"Dazed, or perhaps drunk," Taylor said, framing her eyes against the glass to lessen the glare.

"Well, it *is* Friday night in Raventon," Bobbie said.

Outside, in the restaurant parking lot, a young man, disheveled and dirty, walked in slow, stumbling circles as if confused or lost. He pulled out a pocket watch, checked the time, and resumed a more focused walk.

"Indeed, Friday night in Raventon, Rommy agreed. "Shall we offer *him* a meal?"

"We could, and probably *should,*" Taylor said, "but …"

"But he looks like Crazy Travie's protege," Bobbie finished. "Leave well-enough alone."

"Oh, let's at least ask him. All he can say is 'no'," Taylor said.

23

As the three made their way down Broad Street, they spotted a crowd gathered at the corner of Third and Broad.

"Wonder what's going on down there," Taylor asked.

"No idea," Bobbie answered. "Unless …"

"Ye-e-e-s-s?"

"Unless it's a *Crazy Travie* rally! Park this thing."

"Oh, boy! *Wacky babble!*"

Rommy pulled into one of a few remaining parking spaces in the 300-block. The three ambled out.

"There he is," Bobbie said. "Prepping his sideshow."

"The man definitely draws a crowd," Rommy said. "Has that drum, too."

"He'd still be preaching at Cornerstone Covenant if he hadn't stolen those tithes," Taylor said.

McGuire stopped at the sidewalk apex at the northwest corner of Broad and Third Avenue, as he had done countless Fridays prior. He dropped his two-foot-cubed crate to the concrete. He had made this crate last March, to better accommodate the visibility of his downtown street-preaching, which had become his venue for prophesying and spreading his interpretation of the Word.

Carefully, he stepped atop it. People gathered as he did so, anticipating the Friday-night show, like watching the antics of a 19th-century snake-oil pitchman. The only things missing were an organ and a monkey.

A gust of summer breeze caught McGuire's broad-brimmed, Amish-style hat as he reached for his vest pocket, slapping it for its contents a couple of times. The hat tumbled on a gust and into the crowd.

Clearly frustrated, he pulled two sticks from his back pocket and began tapping the drum.

"Souvenir!" a child shouted, picking the hat from the air as it bounced, and away with it he scampered.

McGuire continued to tap his drum but fixed his stare upon the fleeing young boy, anger shooting from his eyes. He could do little but stare.

"Thief!" shouted McGuire. "That hat's my *collection plate*, boy! Thievery, and ye shall pay, sayeth the Lord! Thou shalt *not* steal! Thou art due a *suffering* and shall thus be *given* it, sayeth the Lord."

The gathering masses laughed. McGuire often concocted scriptural-sounding passages as he spoke, 'thees' and 'thous' added for authenticity, thinking no one would be the wiser. And so began the preaching. A man handed him another hat, for purposes of collecting.

"I want *forty percent!"* the man shouted, handing McGuire the hat, provoking another burst of laughter.

McGuire accepted the hat, acknowledging nothing of the forty percent.

This was only the beginning, spectators knew. McGuire, once a respected man of God and preacher at Cornerstone Covenant Church, was now confined to street-preaching, his sanity ebbing as he aged, ousted by his church those ten years ago after congregants had learned of his own brand of thievery, the taking of thousands of dollars of undeposited tithes from the church treasury, not to mention certain liberties taken with the church's secretary. Congregants had decided not to prosecute McGuire, not wanting to draw attention and make worse a bad situation, especially after having recovered most of the stolen cash found hidden in a jar buried in McGuire's backyard.

McGuire *insisted* he had been set up, the cash taken by parties unknown, perhaps his secretary, he often alleged, the money's "discovery" part of the set-up. Denying the charges in spite of overwhelming circumstantial evidence, he took his fire-breathing brand of spreading his Gospel to the streets of Raventon, injecting his own interpretations of

Scriptures, God-inspired he would say, insisting also that God had anointed him with the gift of prophecy.

McGuire had predicted the return of Christ on four separate occasions, giving exact dates, each of which passed uneventfully into history. In fact, he had predicted the Apocalypse to occur on September 11, 2001, a date which gave some credence to his alleged gift of prophecy, at least in *his* eyes. He preached God's coming wrath, the signs of which, according to McGuire, had been placed clearly by God for all to see.

Folks believed less of what McGuire preached and more of the evidence of a worsening form of dementia displayed by his words and actions. Injecting tongues into his street sermons, he claimed to cast out demons, at the same time condemning such demon-freed young people, while he prophesied the end of the world, the suffering of the masses, with Raventon the epicenter of humanity's downfall.

"James, chapter four, verse fourteen, my brethren!" shouted McGuire. "If you have your Bibles, open to *James 4:14!*"

Nobody had their Bibles. Why bother? This was not church. This was Friday night, and this was theater. People weren't here to be preached to. People were here to be entertained, to consume the snake oil and then spit it out.

"Whereas ye know not what shall be on the morrow," McGuire continued reading. "For what is your life? It is even a vapor, that appeareth for a little time, and then vanisheth away. *Time is of the essence!"*

Again, he tapped his vest pocket. Nothing. He cleared his throat.

"You are here this night, here listening to me, alive you are. But, you could be dead before you get home. God has a death appointment for you, my brethren, and only *He* knows the date and time. In the meanwhile, He will bring suffering into your miserable lives, preparation for your salvation, lessons either you accept or ignore, the latter of which to your eternal peril."

Muted, uncomfortable laughter sprinkled through the crowd. Appreciative patrons, duly satisfied, dropped coins and bills into the hat. This was summertime, Friday-night entertainment in Raventon, GA, and to homefolk the price was worth the paying.

"Make it *fifty* percent, McGuire!" shouted someone.

"I say unto you, 'And as it is appointed unto men once to die, but after this the judgment.' Hebrews nine, verse twenty-seven. Yes, tonight you *eat*, you *drink*, you make *merry*, you even *scoff* at God's Word, but that date, that *time*, looms ahead for *you*, drawing ever nearer, and it will strike when *you* are least expected, like a thief in the night."

"'Beware of *false prophets*,'" shouted another voice, "'which come to you in sheep's clothing, but inwardly they are *ravening wolves*. Matthew seven, verse fifteen.'"

"You believe I am a *ravening wolf*, sir?" McGuire asked.

"You look and sound like a *false* prophet to me, old man," came the answer from an anonymous voice. "You mutate God's Word into lies. So, yes, I suppose by Biblical logic, that makes you a ravening wolf."

"'Tis the Word of the Lord, my friend," McGuire replied. I cannot *change* its truth; I can only *preach* its truth. And we *all must heed* its truth, even *you!*"

"I'll think about heedin soon as I finish this here Pabst!" shouted another voice in the back of the crowd.

Laughter followed. McGuire ignored what he had become accustomed to hearing. He continued.

"Take your Bibles, those of you wise enough to have one on your person, and turn to Mark ten, verse fourteen." He paused a moment and scanned the crowd. "Suffer the little children to come unto me," he read, "and forbid them not: for of such is the kingdom of God. But let's focus on those first four words, 'Suffer the little children'."

The crowd laughed again. "Tap us a marching beat on your drum, Crazy Travie!" came the words of the heckler.

"Children *must suffer* if they are to receive salvation," McGuire shouted. And we are *all* God's children, and thus we must *all* suffer."

"I think we're *all* experiencing a bit of that suffering right now, old man!"

The cash tossed and dropped into the hat grew to overflowing. Raventonians appreciated a good show, especially a live show, regardless of the show's content. The crowd became just as much a part of that show as was McGuire.

McGuire bent to retrieve the hat, taking the cash and stuffing it into his pocket. His take, he knew without counting, met his expectations and would provide his sustenance for the coming week. He reached again for his empty vest pocket, tapping it without his own notice, it seemed, as if by instinct or some robotic obligation. Without another word, he gathered his crate and drum and started for home.

"See you next Friday, Preacher McGuire," some shouted.

"I must go to Miss Peasy's house," he whispered. "Sterling's there. I *feel* it. I *know* it. I *must* get that watch!"

"Show's over, I suppose," Rommy said.

The crowd dispersed, mostly. Two men lingered, giving their silent attention to McGuire but for reasons others could never imagine. Keeping a distance safe from notice, they followed McGuire home, jotting notes as they walked.

"Let's get over to Music and More," Taylor said. "We have just enough time before they close. I really want to get that D-28."

"Really in a hurry, aren't you?" Bobbie asked, smiling.

"I guess I am. Don't understand why. I usually sleep on such decisions as this."

"Yeah, I imagine this decision's going to cost you a few grand," Rommy said.

"About *three* grand," Taylor replied. "Worth every penny. Let's go!"

24

Dravik Kryzinkov was a master of disguise, having served in the Soviet Army for two decades before the take-down of the Wall, as well as service as an operative in the Federal Intelligence Service of the Russian Federation. His tenure in the states was short thus far, just shy of eight months, having recently completed unauthorized acquisitions of intellectual properties from AI companies located in Atlanta and Sacramento. Lucrative work, opportunities that rivaled drugs and guns, even that of artificial intelligence, remained for him to complete, assuring an extension of his undocumented status in the United States.

He and his associate, Vladimir Provich, a Soviet-era medical doctor now practicing in Atlanta, had been tasked with procuring human organs for exclusive use by Russian diplomats and their families. Neither man was averse to stepping outside the scope of their mission by procuring some of those harvested organs for distribution to elements of the Russian black market, working hand-in-hand with American counterparts, one of which resided in Raventon and practiced at Raventon Mercy Hospital, a Doctor Pernell Cromwell. The two were responsible for expediting the shipment of procured organs to points within the U.S. and abroad.

Locations and personnel for carrying out this illegal and macabre black-market procurement, which heretofore had been beyond the scrutiny of authorities, became increasingly difficult to maintain. Centralized sites needed utmost secrecy. The use of qualified physicians had to be secured under the tightest vetting and airtight incentives, mostly in the form of financial payments and promises of personal protection. Nothing could be left to chance.

But the Austin, Texas operational hub had been compromised. Three of Dravik's associates had been killed, two of those three by Dravik's hand, just to prevent any leakage of incriminating information.

A new location had been found. Raventon, Georgia was located at the center of the Birmingham-Chattanooga-Atlanta triangle of medical expertise and such essential resources as quick access to international air travel. It was here Dravik set up his latest operations. But he needed a physical site, a site in plain sight, a site thus inconspicuous by its docile surroundings. He had found it. But the competition must first be neutralized.

Dravik had observed and recorded Preacher McGuire's religious performances on Broad Street, week after week, making mental notes of his speech patterns, his mannerisms, his dress, his dialect, his syntax and semantics, anything integral to *becoming* Travis McGuire.

He knew of McGuire's involvement in the cases of those eight missing teens from 2013, eight teens whom McGuire had lured into his house and had slaughtered in the process of conducting his own transplantation experiments. All that was not known was where McGuire had disposed of the bodies. He knew as well that all suspicion of McGuire had been dismissed, his name cleared, the charges fully discounted and thrown out, all in deference to suspicion deftly redirected to Miss Peasy Parlevous. The public wanted it no other way.

Dravik knew if the charade of McGuire's shadowy operations had worked then, and it had, including his feigned defense of Miss Peasy, Dravik's own charade would continue to work now. He knew townsfolk now considered McGuire nothing more than a harmless oddity, perhaps in the throes of worsening dementia and incapable of anything genuinely nefarious. Dravik understood all of this, a scenario almost too good to be true and a perfect facade for his continuing operations.

But Dravik knew another truth. The real McGuire would have to go. Working his operations from the relative anonymity of McGuire's basement lately had become too risky. McGuire was prone to roam his house, to venture unexpectedly down the basement stairs and at such times most inopportune to Dravik's and Vladimir's own ghastly work of organ harvesting. Concealment had become awkward and inefficient.

Hence Dravik's detailed study of McGuire's persona. Neutralizing McGuire was the easy part. The difficult part was in *becoming* McGuire, in executing a seamless transition into McGuire himself and without the slightest bit of suspicion. Dravik had done this before, all over the world.

25

Preacher McGuire occupied a nineteenth-century, two-story antebellum home in midtown Raventon, its construction predating all the Victorian-era homes surrounding it. Few ever witnessed McGuire coming to or going from the house. The common presumption was that he owned the home free and clear, had for decades, despite his apparent infrequent presence, as opposed to merely squatting on the property.

The clapboard house had no obvious signs of electricity or running water. On infrequent occasions, a line of smoke lifted from one of the house's two chimneys, suggesting his presence. That and the occasional light of candles drifting from room to room gave the only reasons to believe anyone spent any appreciable time there, other than ghosts, perhaps.

Neighbors had complained about the unkempt yard, its discolored grass and its patches of crabgrass, dandelions, and other plentiful weeds, its uncontrolled mounds of fire ants and neglected litter scattered about.

Because McGuire had no official criminal record, along with the fact the man possessed a certain entertainment charisma, authorities did not pursue remedies for his odd behavior, believing his eccentricities age-related and thus posed no real threat to the public.

Conversations concerning the man were spoken in whispers, mainly among neighbors, such words which filtered their way into the community rumor mill for processing and consumption. Folk shared disturbing observations over the years, observations of McGuire receiving visitors after dark, mostly adults but a few children as well, none of whom were ever seen leaving this house. Coincidence, perhaps, until the numbers of missing persons noticeably increased, particularly those of children.

Miss Peasy absorbed the public blame for the missing-persons incidences, despite the absurdity of blaming a physically exhausted, elderly woman. Her peculiarities as the public's Witch of Raventon nonetheless fueled the speculation.

Two men, Dravik and Vladimir, among McGuire's audience to the preaching of suffering and sacrifice, decided the time had come to pay him an in-person visit. And so tomorrow they would.

26

Saturday morning,
9:30AM
July 5, 2020

"Come *in*, Taylor! So happy to see you again. How's college?"

"Couldn't be better, Miss Peasy. I appreciate you allowing me over. And it's so good to see *you* again. You're looking well and … wait, is that what I *think* it is?"

"If you're thinking it's a fresh-from-the-oven apple pie, then *yes!* Want a slice?"

"More than I want my *next breath!*"

"Let it cool a bit first."

"Sounds great. Did I say you're looking well?"

"For ninety-eight, perhaps. I think I'm way past the 'looking well' part, but thank you for your sweet words, Taylor." Miss Peasy noticed the guitar hanging on Taylor's shoulder. "Buy a guitar, did you?"

"Yes, last evening, as a matter of fact, from Music and More. It's a Martin D-28. I've had this inexplicable urge lately to learn Civil War camp songs, marching songs. Weird, huh? I'm thinking it comes from exposure to my dad's constant history discussions."

"He *is* quite the buff," Miss Peasy said with a wry wink. "Civil War, that is. So, play me a tune."

"Oh, I don't know if I'm ready for that yet. Maybe in—"

"Go ahead, sweetie. Play me one."

Taylor smiled uncomfortably but could not refuse. The urge to play was too strong and Miss Peasy was too cute.

"Well, then, let's see," Taylor said, swinging the Martin off her shoulder as she sat. She strummed a few chords and twisted a few keys to adjust for proper tuning.

"Sing it, too, if you don't mind, Taylor. Your voice is so sweet."

Taylor smiled. "Here's an old, familiar Southern song, written by a Northerner, so I'm told," Taylor said. "It's always haunted me." She began playing its introduction.

Miss Peasy smiled upon hearing the mellow opening notes, played softly, eloquently, by Taylor's measured plucks. She sighed. "You play it so well."

"Thank you, Miss Peasy," Taylor replied. "Just a few Cs, Fs, and Gs; nothing complicated."

"Maybe not to you. Sterling's favorite, 'Dixie'," Miss Peasy noted, "that and 'Lorena', as he mentioned both in his letters and in his message he brought to me this morning."

"Oh, I wish I was in the land of cotton, old times there are not forgotten ...". Then it hit her. Taylor stopped playing. "Wait ... *what?* His message *brought* to you ... *this morning,* Miss Peasy? Brought to you by ..."

"Why, yes, by Sterling himself. Actually, I can't say Sterling *delivered* it."

"Whew!" Taylor said, happy to hear Miss Peasy acknowledge reality. "I thought for a minute that…"

"Here 'tis. Sterling found this for me among the many letters and mementos in this box filled with such. Read this."

Miss Peasy handed the letter to Taylor.

"*Did* he, now?"

She propped her guitar against the sofa and took the letter from Miss Peasy's hand.

"Read it aloud for me, Taylor dear," Miss Peasy said.

"Certainly," Taylor replied, carefully opening the letter's folds. Taylor read,

> July 4, 1863
>
> Union field hospital
>
> Dearest Peasy Parlevous,
>
> "'My name is Sterling Vice. I was born January, 1827, in Spartanburg, SC. My family moved to Raventon, Georgia in the spring of 1835, living there until early 1850, whereupon we moved to Wedowee, Alabama after my daddy had purchased

a hundred acres of prime bottomland along the Wedowee Creek. It was in Wedowee that I was befriended by your great-great uncle, Henry Iverson. Henry and I worked as blacksmiths and gunsmiths in Wedowee until the summer of 1861, when Henry decided his devotion to country overruled his own pursuit of wealth and comfort. That is when Henry decided to join the 7th Georgia regiment and pursue instead the defense and independence of our new nation, the Confederate States of America. Henry always was the idealist, and his heart belonged to Georgia.

"'I followed suit, after a couple of years of deliberative introspection, in early spring of '63, walking northward toward Raventon. Following a short stint there, I departed for Lee's army, taking with me a 12-year-old orphaned boy, his idealistic sights set on being a rebel drummer for Robert E. Lee. We walked through the mountains of North Carolina and western Virginia to Richmond, whereupon we were directed toward the crossroads community of Chancellorsville, Virginia and Lee's Army of Northern Virginia.

"'Turns out Lee's Army, by the time we had reached them, was fully engaged in a God-awful fight at Chancellorsville, Virginia. I and the lad participated briefly in that battle, fighting with Jackson's Corps, surprising the Union XI Corps on that army's right flank, pushing it off the field, out of the fight, shattering it.

"'I was blessed to have survived the desperate infantry firefights that followed on that day and on May 3, after which we headed northward into Pennsylvania to once again take the fighting out of a war-ravaged South and into the North's homeland.

"'It was at the small town of Gettysburg, Pennsylvania that the great battle was fought and where I, by God's Grace, was reunited with Henry.

"'Much has been made by Raventonians since that battle about how Henry shamefully ran from the enemy, how he fled from his duty, fled from his countrymen, at the climax of Pickett's Charge, near the stone wall at the Angle. That conclusion, as you know, was drawn from the fact he was shot in the back, killed by Yankee infantry, presumably as he fled in shame from the field of honor.

"'It should be noted that many men of both sides received wounds in their backs, simply from the nature of the fight, the unpredictable swirl of battle, men turning to address crises coming at them from all directions. Most wounds to the back had nothing to do with any lack of courage. But soldiers' witness accounts carry not only the credibility they often deserve, perspectives that historians can miss, but sometimes the inaccuracies of the fog of war that, unfortunately, find refuge in their accounts of battle.

"'Your family throughout the generations has suffered the slings and arrows, the total humiliation of these accusations of cowardice cast upon Henry, many of which continued forward with the generations. I have witnessed such disgrace that has befallen your family and you. I have been sent to finally put the matter to rest and to restore Henry's honor, your family's name, and your peace. I am here to dispel the lies and to let you know the truth of what happened that hot day, July 3, 1863, during the great charge of General

George Pickett's, General Isaac Trimble's, and General James Pettigrew's divisions upon the Union lines on Cemetery Ridge.

"'Please allow me into your home the morning of July 5, 2020 so that the truth can finally receive the glow of light and the clarity of right it so deserves. Only then can reputations and honor be restored.

"'You have in your possession among the body of the letters of Henry and myself, my final letter, written on July 5, 1863, as I lay wounded in a Union field hospital. I dictated this letter to my attending nurse, her name not known by me, as my wounds and deteriorating condition prevented my writing it myself. This letter presents my real-time account of the battle of July 3, 1863 and of the heroics of Henry Iverson and Charlie Dyer, both of whom selflessly saved my life during the battle.

"'My sincerest respects to you, I am your devoted,

Sterling Vice"

Speechless, Taylor stared another minute at the faded words on the yellowed document, gathering what few coherent thoughts she might.

"Are those … those boxes the relics and letters and such from Henry," Taylor asked with a sigh, pointing.

"Yes. Sterling's, too."

Taylor bent to get a closer look and to touch these priceless time travelers.

"This is fascinating, Miss Peasy, your collection of Civil War records and relics," Taylor said, holding the shot Bible. "You must be very proud."

"Proud? That's an *understatement*."

"Is the Raventon Beacon aware of this, aware of these letters, your collection?"

"No, 'fraid not."

"Well, it's high time they were made aware, don't you think? When do you expect … Sterling?"

"This evening, but he gave no specific time."

"Did he deliver this letter to you in person?"

"As I said, he did not deliver it, per se, but he did pick it from the bunch here, as if he knew all along where it was. Might as well have delivered it himself. Otherwise, I likely would have never known it existed."

"But … you did not actually … *see* him."

"Why, *yes*, I *did* actually see him. He was standing right *here*, by my tea tray after I got home from doing my banking business."

Taylor's red-flag, hold-everything! sense sparked forth.

"Miss Peasy, you … he was standing *here*, *inside* your house … *here* by your tea tray?"

"Well, I believe that any spirit from the mid-nineteenth century can pretty much go through any wall it desires, don't you?" Miss Peasy chuckled.

"Miss Peasy, this letter claims a date of July 4, 1863, yet it contains a present-day perspective, as well as knowledge of the grief you and your family have suffered. How is that possible, if the letter's genuine? I really don't—"

"Now, now, Taylor, let's not be negative about this. I understand your doubts. I got a few of my own. Just in case, mind you, I got my nine-millimeter right here under my sofa pillow." Miss Peasy winked and smiled. "A spirit's not going to be intimidated by that, of course, but it can sure put the fear of God into a mortal imposter."

Both sat. Taylor opened the Bible to where the bullet rested lodged these one hundred and fifty-seven years. She looked around, half-expecting Sterling's spirit to appear despite her competing feelings of a firm-yet-quivering faith in Miss Peasy's word and her abject skepticism of the truth of a latter-day Sterling and the authenticity of his supposed letter, knowing better the silliness the former presented and utter preposterous impossibility of the latter. Taylor's faith in the soundness of Miss Peasy's mind now faced its supreme test.

Miss Peasy, meanwhile, puffed mightily on her briarwood, smoke curling with her confidence carried by the humid air in every direction, as if giving form to its own spirit, her eyes dancing side to side, widened with full expectation, watchful of the front door and Sterling's anticipated arrival.

Taylor read again Sterling's letter, silently. Her eyes acknowledged astonishment with every word.

He even picked this specific date? she thought.

Taylor wanted to place a call to the Raventon Police Department to request an officer keep a watchful eye, but she resisted for now.

"July 5, Miss Peasy," Taylor whispered upon finishing her second reading. "2020. That's … *today.* How could Sterling know in 1863, if that's when this letter was written, that *you* would be here now, *here today?* How could he know you would exist at all?"

"I can't explain the things of the divinely supernatural, the divinely inspired, Taylor. He's coming back this evening, like he said. I just *know* he is, and I want a witness. *You.*"

"The same Sterling Vice that fought with Lee at Gettysburg, that lived in Raventon, that … that *died* … presumably a *hundred and fifty-seven years ago. That* Sterling Vice?"

"The very same Sterling Vice."

"But, *me?*" Taylor placed the Bible on the coffee table, concerned Miss Peasy had finally "gone 'round the bend" toward which she often claimed her aging mind was taking her. "Why do you want *me* here, Miss Peasy? This sounds more like a personal family matter."

"Because you and I are close, Taylor, just *like* family, and I trust you. I know that within your skepticism is a receptive heart, a willingness to listen, to reserve judgment, to *learn*."

"I say this with all respect, Miss Peasy, because you know I love you and would do anything for you … but have you considered the possibility that *this* Sterling Vice is no more than--"

"A figment of my ripe and ancient imagination? Indeed, I have, Taylor, and I can assure you his presence and voice were as real to me as you standing before me, as real as the apple pie in my oven and the pipe on my tray, the very tray itself. Yes, I am ninety-eight years old, but my mind is as sharp as a razor."

"Well, yes, I'm sure, Miss Peasy, but what if he's a *con* job, an imposter preying on an eld--, a senior citizen?"

"An *elderly* woman like me?" Miss Peasy sipped her tea and smiled. "First thing I thought about, Taylor, *first* thing."

Miss Peasy reached inside the wooden box and retrieved from the multitude of letters a framed tintype photograph. She looked at it a moment and sighed, handing the image to Taylor.

"I was as much a skeptic as you. Look here. This's an 1862 tintype of Sterling Vice. Found it in a small wooden case among the other documents and relics. Sterling suggested that I compare his visage to the tintype. How would he know I had such a picture, a tintype of all things, if he were *not* the genuine article? No one has seen the contents of these boxes for over fifty years. In fact, I am the last living family member to know of these relics, and I haven't said a word of them to anyone since they were handed over to me those many decades ago.

"So, I compared that tintype photograph, *this* photograph, to him as he stood before me. He was wearing the *same* clothing, Taylor, no worse for wear, for age, or for the conditions he wore this clothing back in '63. Some blood stains on the left shoulder and left sleeve. A bit dirtier and battle-smudged, perhaps. Now how do you explain that? *This,"* Miss Peasy emphasized, "is the man who came to visit me this morning."

Taylor took the tintype and gasped. "*This* is the man who visited you this morning?"

"Yes. *This* is the man. Do you doubt me still?"

"No, I ... Because we -- Bobbie, Rommy, and I - saw *this* man wandering the streets last Friday evening, looking as dazed as a stray puppy. Only difference was that he was wearing a slouch hat, a tear along the left rim, and his left shoulder was bandaged, the arm in a sling. Every ... everything else -- shirt, suspenders, coat, *all* of it - is *identical.* Like you said, *same* clothing, only dirtier. We thought he was a drifter, a homeless man, and offered him some food, but he refused. He said he had come for one thing and one thing only, to find ... *you.*

"We initially brushed him off as maybe intoxicated. But since he had mentioned you by name, I thought it prudent to keep a watchful eye on you and your house.

"So … *this* is Sterling Vice, Gettysburg veteran, eh."

27

"So he says. And I believe him. I *have* to believe him. I'm ninety-eight years old, Taylor, and I've always been a risk-taker. Might as well roll the dice on this one, too. Can't change that about me *now*, can I?

"He told me he had some news for me, some news I'd want to hear regarding my great-great grandmama's son, Henry Iverson, born in 1831, also a veteran of the battle of Gettysburg and the very reason my family has suffered all these generations at the hands of unforgiving Southern traditionalists. Henry, the story goes - and believe me, I am reminded *constantly* of how that story goes -- was killed in that battle, shot in the back, *running away,* during Pickett's Charge; they say he was a coward. Henry's alleged cowardice was the root of my being labeled as the Witch of Raventon."

"Why did folks label *you* the Witch of Raventon, Miss Peasy? Why was his cowardice *your* fault?"

"*Alleged* cowardice. As for the Witch of Raventon moniker, why *not*, is probably the better question. Their firm belief in my ancestors' disloyalty to the Southern Cause, their infectious derision of me, of my family's name, was relentless. Such derision was passed down generation to generation, like some mutation of genetic code. I was the latest in a long line ostracized at every turn, which is the main reason I took up flying, to take me *above* and *away* from all the craziness. Folks likened my love of flying to a witch riding a broomstick, and my isolation didn't help matters.

"Things got worse when I played along with the 'witch' hysteria. Playfully, with maybe a dash of vengeance, I cast 'curses' upon certain folks I despised with equal fervor for their cruelties, nothing more than simple waves of my hands and a growl or two, harmless stuff but enough to make 'em jump. They *believed* I was a witch, so I *became* that witch. Give the folks what they want, leave 'em laughin or screamin, I suppose.

"Thing is, some of those same folks started *disappearing*, even dying off unexpectedly, teenagers especially. I was accused of black magic, *murder* even. Preacher McGuire defended my honor, but his reputation and his own troubles made any defense of his problematic and ineffective. At least he *seemed* an advocate.

"Of course, they could not pin any evidence on me because *there was no evidence* of any crime having been committed. Not by *me*, anyhow. My theory about some of those cases is that perhaps some crimes, indeed, *were* committed, by those with grudges against those who disappeared, those who died, by the likes of those, perhaps, who kidnapped a young girl's dad and hid him in a cave," Miss Peasy said in reference to Taylor's dad and her adventure with the Chamber of Skulls, "and they used the common knowledge of the Witch of Raventon label to make me look the guilty party. Public opinion can be a cruel dispenser of false justice."

"But how can this man who claims to be Sterling Vice actually *be* the Sterling Vice from the *mid-19th century*. That's a leap of faith the most fervent of my Baptist upbringing won't allow me to accept, Miss Peasy."

"I know, sweet Taylor, and I accept your disbelief. But I do also believe you will be an *honest* witness, and I *do* believe your mind will be open to change."

KNOCK ... KNOCK ... KNOCK.

"Must be him, Taylor."

"Let me get the door, Miss Peasy."

"Thank you, Taylor." Miss Peasy eased herself into her wicker chair and took flame to her tobacco. She held the bullet-shot Bible in one hand and rested the tintype on her lap. The thought crossed her mind that all of this was God's way of preparing her for her appointment with the hereafter.

28

"Mornin, ma'am," Sterling said with a tip of his hat, a broad smile lighting is face. "My name is—"

"Yes, I know. Sterling Vice. Let's get one thing straight, Mr. Vice."

Nervously, Sterling removed his hat and placed it back onto his head. "So, I reckon Miss Peasy's told you about me."

"Indeed, she has. And, I and my friends saw you roaming aimlessly around Raventon the other night; tried to give you a bite to eat." Taylor studied Sterling for a moment. "But you turned us away. I must admit, you *are* the spitting image of the tintype Miss Peasy showed me. And she *does* believe you have somehow crossed the great divide of time and immortality to come to her. *Me*, well, I'm not so convinced. Call me a 21st-century skeptic."

"I understand, ma'am. But how would I know about the *letters* she possesses, *my* letters, those of Henry's? How would I know *she* had the Bible, shot almost through, ball still lodged in its pages, even the verse that stopped it, if I weren't *the* Sterling Vice? *How* would I know about the tintype? I have never been in this house before."

"Once, you have," Taylor corrected. "Memory *that* short, Mr. Vice? This morning, before Miss Peasy arrived home."

Sterling could not deny this one exception.

"You are correct; I was here this morning. I meant before today. You'll have to accept my word of honor that I have never pried into her belongings, today or ever. I waited for her to return."

"I'll check with Miss Peasy about that. Answer me this, Mr. Vice."

"If I can."

"What verse in that shot Bible did the bullet stop, the verse you referenced in one of your letters and again just now referenced?"

"That would be Isaiah 48:9, ma'am. I could never forget that verse. 'For my own name's sake, I delay my wrath; for the sake of my praise I hold it back from you, so as not to destroy you completely.'

"Protected me at Gettysburg, this scripture, through the battle anyway, in that hellish wheat field and in that blasted charge on that third day. The power of this scripture gave Henry the courage to do what he did, to keep the protection alive, to save my life, as Charlie had done by giving me his watch and by taking bullets meant for me. I lay on a bunk, wounded, my shoulder and arm burning with pain. There was ... there was an ... explosion. Before or after I had died, I cannot say. And then I found myself resurrected, wandering around in this remarkably strange world of a 21st-century Raventon. That's when I learned of my mission."

"Your *mission*?"

"You will soon learn of it, too."

Taylor heard his recitation of Isaiah 48:9, the measured flow of the words, the sincerity of his tone. If he were a con man trying to take advantage of Miss Peasy, he was either not playing the part well or he was playing it brilliantly. Still not wholly convinced this entity had stepped in fleshly form across the divide of time from 1863 to 2020, she was no longer *un*convinced either.

"Mr. Vice, you are *not* Jesus."

"No, ma'am, I am certainly not. My only point is that resurrection *is* possible, if the Lord so wills it."

"Well, yes, but--"

"May we step inside, Taylor Smart?"

"You know my name?"

"There are many things I never imagined I would know."

"You … you may step inside, Mr. Vice," Taylor said with hesitation, "but understand you are being watched, scrutinized with utmost deliberation at this very moment, and if you *are* flesh and blood, as I believe you *must* be, any move of ill-intent on your part will be met with deadly force."

"I understand, and I thank you," Sterling said, again removing his hat. "I assure you I am who I say I am, as well as whence I claim to have come. I am here *only* to correct a gross error in Miss Peasy's family history, after which you and she will never see me again, at least not on this plane. There no longer will be the need."

"Somehow, that worries me," Taylor said, thinking that thieves have a way of disappearing with the goods, permanently.

29

Miss Peasy stoked the burn of her pipe, her excitement emitting a steady pounding, an outpouring of smoke, as would a locomotive. Her eyes brightened and she smiled, nearly allowing the pipe to drop.

"Come in, *come in*. Take a seat, Sterling, Taylor. Help yourself to some tea."

"Thank you, ma'am," Sterling said, sitting. "Won't be needin any right now."

Taylor sat, just as the doorbell rang.

"Probably Rommy. I asked him last evening to meet me here today."

"Good, good!" Miss Peasy said. "This is turning into a regular reunion. I must get us some pie."

"I'll get the door," Taylor said.

Taylor walked toward the door, once or twice turning to sneak another disbelieving peek at Sterling Vice. Miss Peasy said something to Sterling, inaudible to Taylor, but Sterling laughed. Taylor smiled, her acceptance of this alternative reality growing.

Taylor opened the door. She gasped.

"Preacher McGuire! What … what are *you* doing here?"

"Came to check on Miss Peasy," he said. "I … I saw a strange man enter her home this morning, and I wanted to make sure she was well."

"Oh, she's *quite* well, sir. Quite well. You … saw a strange man enter?"

"May I come in?"

"Well … I … yes, I suppose it's okay."

"Thank you."

The two entered into Miss Peasy's parlor.

Sterling's eyes widened.

"*You!*" Sterling said.

"Indeed, 'tis I. Good to see you again, Vice. Been a long time … in a worldly sense, that is. You left in *such* a hurry, it seems you left with something of mine."

"It is *not* yours, McGuire!" Sterling replied. "It was *never* yours!"

"What are you two talking about?" Miss Peasy asked. "How do you know this man, Travis?"

"Show them, Vice. Show them what we're … talking about."

Sterling pulled from his pocket a gold-lidded pocket watch.

"A *pocket watch*, Sterling?" Miss Peasy asked.

"*My* pocket watch, ma'am," McGuire insisted. "Took it from me one hundred fifty-seven years ago as I tended his wounds after the battle of Gettysburg. Yes, Taylor, I was a Union surgeon during the Civil War. Lord, the *twists* life can take."

"A *Union sur …*", Taylor said.

"Don't look so surprised, woman," McGuire said. "I'm sure that by now Sterling has told you all about his journey."

"Well, *yes* ... but I ..."

"I devised ways to transplant certain human organs and bones into wounded Union soldiers, such medical expertise well ahead of its time. Unfortunately, I was not able to devote the necessary time to fulfilling such time-consuming surgeries, as the number of wounded men overwhelmed our hospitals, and, well, the necessary resources just were not yet available. But, they are now. And they shall evermore be. Sterling and I had equal possession of this watch in that field hospital when a rebel shell struck in our midst, taking me out of physical existence. Sterling, if I remember correctly, had already passed."

"Killed, that is?" Taylor asked.

"Both of us, dead," McGuire answered, "and thus both of us were resurrected into this point in time, each with his own mission and purpose."

"And your purpose?" Taylor asked.

"To perfect my transplantation methodologies, using 21st-century knowledge and specimens, to take that expertise back to 1863 battlefields ... and, of course, to investors who will pay wildly for such knowledge and expertise."

"Specimens!" Taylor exclaimed. "What, exactly, do you mean by … 'specimens'?"

"How could I have taken something *from* you that *wasn't yours* to begin with, McGuire?" Sterling asked.

"I won't argue with you, Vice. It was given to me, I possessed it, and you took it. Give me the watch and you'll never see me again. You're heaven-bound anyway! What do you care about some watch?"

"The watch belonged to Charlie Dyer, an orphaned drummer boy I took under my wing in Raventon before we headed north to join Lee's army. Charlie gave me the watch as we marched across that open field, under intense fire. Said he *needed* to give it to me, to trust him. I did, and now I know why. He later died, shielding me with his body during Pickett's Charge. This watch once belonged to Joseph O. Neal, the great 19th-century evangelist and divine healer who claimed to possess the gift of resurrection. Obviously, he possessed such a divine gift, at least his *watch* did, for here we are. This watch is embodied with that divine power for its possessor, which is why Charlie wanted *me* to have it.

"You'll not get this watch, McGuire. This is one spoil of war you never deserved and shall *never* possess."

What is happening here? Taylor thought. *Where is Rommy?*

"Boys, *boys!*" Miss Peasy said. "I must ask you to leave, Preacher McGuire."

"*Doctor* McGuire, Miss Peasy," McGuire said, turning to Sterling. "I'll leave. But I'll get my watch's worth, make no mistake. Working on that *now*, by the way. Full resurrection shall be *mine!*"

"Full resurrection?" Taylor said, puzzled.

McGuire opened the front door, slamming it behind him, standing silent on the porch, pondering his next move.

30

Saturday morning,
July 5, 2020
9:16AM

Silby Johnson pedaled his bicycle down East Fourth Street, weaving around parked cars and dodging squirrels darting across his path. Ahead, he noticed an old man, Preacher McGuire perhaps, though he could not discern from this distance against the bevy of life-sized, similar-looking Halloween props still left scattered throughout the neighborhood from last year. No prop, this man indeed looked exactly like Preacher McGuire, standing on the corner, his cane lifted and waving to get Silby's attention. But this was not McGuire. This was Dravik Kryzinkov, master of disguise.

"Wonder what Mr. McGuire wants with me?" Silby asked, braking his bike and turning toward McGuire. He coasted to a stop.

"Silby, my boy, did you read your Bible today?" he asked. Dravik had made meticulous notes about many of Raventon's residents.

"Yes, sir, as usual. You need me for something?"

"Matter of fact I do. Need you to make a delivery."

"Delivery?"

"On your bike. To 813 South Walnut. There will be a man waiting for you to give him this bag. No delays, no venturing off to other places. Go straight to 813 Walnut. But do not pedal fast. I need you to be very careful to protect the contents of this bag. Do you understand?"

"Yes, but I've got to get home for lunch. We're having roast beef and mashed potatoes. Gravy, too. I love gravy on my mashed potatoes, don't you, Preacher McGuire?"

"A hundred dollars, boy. You ought to do it for free. Don't you *want* to do the Lord's work?"

Silby Johnson turned thirteen last month. As a six-year-old, he had reported to the police, via his mom, strange sounds, screaming sounds, coming from inside the McGuire house back in October of 2013, the same year those eight teens came up missing. Silby's reports were little believed at first, especially because of the community's common knowledge of his mentally-challenged condition, not to mention Silby's young, imagination-filled age those seven years ago.

"Lord's work?"

"Just like you young people to *question* the work of the Lord. Just as you do your daily Bible reading, you must *also* do the Lord's work as He *presents* it to you to do, even if it means sacrifice and suffering and inconvenience. Even if it means deferring the roast beef."

"Well … I reckon I can do this. 'Bout how long you s'pect it'll take, Preacher McGuire?"

"Not long, I'm sure. But first, I need you to clean a piece of furniture for me."

"Clean?"

"But I need you to do it *now*. No time for going home first or telling your friends. This is a *special* opportunity for you and you only. Come with me now, and there's a hundred dollars waiting for you."

"How long to clean the furniture?"

"So many questions! Just one piece. About thirty minutes, I suppose, and another thirty to make the delivery and report back to me for your payment. The man will give you a receipt for the bag, and I need you to bring me back that receipt. Spare *me* -- spare the *Lord*, rather -- an hour of your time, boy."

"A hundred dollars, you say?" Silby said, smiling, pondering. "Ain't never seen *that* much money before. There *is* a video game or two I'd like to get." He paused a few more seconds. "Okay, Mr. McGuire, you got yourself a delivery boy."

"And a furniture cleaner."

"Yes, sir."

"Then, let's go."

Silby followed the old man down the street several houses. No words were exchanged until the two arrived at the foot of the hill of McGuire's house.

"I gotta admit to you, Mr. McGuire," Silby said, gazing up toward the house, "you got the *spookiest* house in all of Raventon. No offense, of course. It's a cool house."

"None taken, boy. It is a might spooky looking." He smiled. "Age'll do that, you know. Now let's get you to cleaning that piece of furniture."

The old man—rather, Dravik, the old man's replacement—led Silby down the basement stairs, guided only by Dravik's flashlight. As the two reached the basement floor, Dravik flipped the light switch. Before them, looming ten feet tall and half hidden by shadows, was that piece of furniture, a *guillotine*, its polished-steel blade hoisted high, like the open jaw of a T-rex, its potential energy poised to strike.

"Wow, Mr. McGuire!" Silby managed through his awe. "I ain't *never* seen no *guillotine* before, not in real life, anyway."

The guillotine blade was stained with trails of blood, as were the lunettes, the basket, and the floor. Mouth agape, Silby stared at the machine.

"One thing you need to be mindful of, boy. See that switch about halfway up the side beam?"

"Yes, sir."

"That's the blade trigger. Do not, under *any* circumstances, touch that trigger. Doing so will release the blade, which just might take off your arm or such."

"How … how do I clean the blade, sir?"

"Use this ladder. There is a bucket of cleaning solvent and water at the top of the ladder. Scrub the blade thoroughly, as well as the lunettes below. And watch the rope. It can tangle, getting in the way of the blade's path."

"Lunettes?"

"Where the head … or whatever … is placed to await the blade's fall."

"What … what …?" Silby started.

"Question, boy?"

Silby then noticed the several animal head mounts on the basement walls, and he remembered seeing more on the walls upstairs. He figured the guillotine must have been used for quick and clean animal head removals. Dravik had predicted Silby -- any boy chosen for the task -- would make that convenient connection.

"Nothing, sir. I'll get right to it."

"Good. When you are done, come upstairs for the bag and its delivery. I will have it ready for you. Remember, a hundred dollars."

A hundred dollars. That was more money than Silby earned for ten months' worth of allowances.

"Better get started," Silby said as Dravik disappeared up the basement stairs. "Say, that McGuire is looking a might thin these days. Lost some weight, I reckon. Makes him look taller than I remember, too, even younger. Ain't got near the slouch he used to have. Oh, well. Good for him."

Twenty-five minutes later, Silby emerged upstairs. Dravik stood tall in the den, watching the basement door in anticipation of Silby's arrival.

"All done, sir."

"Did you get it *all?"*

"Think so. Looks spotless to me."

"We will check it out together when you return. Here is the bag. Hurry, but be very careful."

"What's *in* this thing? Pretty heavy."

"Not for you to worry about. Your payment is for delivery, not curiosity. Just you be careful."

"I will, Mr. McGuire," Silby said, taking the bag. "By the way, you're looking much thinner these days. Eating better, I reckon?"

Dravik had not considered the weight differences between McGuire and himself, a rare neglect of detail.

"Eating better, yes. Thank you for noticing."

"You look *taller*. Maybe you need some mashed potatoes, too." Silby smiled. "Be back in a little bit."

Silby mounted his bike, the bag's strap secure on his right shoulder, and started off, quickly gaining speed. He curved around the intersection and vanished in the shadows of oaks that lined the street's sidewalks.

Ahead, he noticed Rommy and Bobbie walking hand in hand.

"Hey, Silby!" Bobbie shouted.

"Hey, Bobbie, Rommy," Silby said through his gasping. "Can't stop to talk. Gotta deliver this bag. But, you ought to see the *guillotine* in Preacher McGuire's basement! It's really *cool*. Looks like something out of the *French Revolution*. Probably as *old* as that, too. Uses it for his animal head mounts, he says. Ha! Let's hope that's its purpose. I just now finished cleaning all the blood off it. Sure looks like it is, its purpose, I mean, from all the head mounts hanging in that house. Well, gotta scoot! I'll be seeing you!"

Silby pulled away, accelerating as he sailed downhill.

"Did he say … *guillotine?*" Bobbie asked.

"And blood. That's what I heard, too," Rommy replied. "So, are you feeling any better?"

"A bit, maybe. Still achy, and my throat's sore."

Rommy held his palm against Bobbie's forehead. "Still feverish. Let me get you home. I'll phone Taylor and let her know that we'll have to cancel tonight's bowling."

"Taylor told me she was going over to Miss Peasy's. Something about making sure that strange fellow we saw Friday night hasn't actually tried to approach Miss Peasy. Plus, she's going to help sort through some of her Civil War relics, letters and diaries and such. Might want to see if she's still there."

"Yes, she told me that as well," Rommy replied. "Thanks. I'll call her."

31

Rommy took Bobbie home, gave her some Tylenol, and told her he would check back later. He called Taylor to tell her about the guillotine Silby had mentioned, wanting to know if she was aware of such a device owned by McGuire.

"Hey, Tay, I—What? Yes, she's not feeling well. She's resting. Have to cancel tonight's bowling date."

"Okay. I wasn't in much of a mood for bowling anyway."

"Wanted to ask you about something," Rommy said.

"Shoot."

"We ran into Silby Johnson a little while ago. Said he had just been to McGuire's house and had - now get this -- had just *cleaned* his ... *guillotine*."

"His ... *what?*"

"You heard me right, his *guillotine.* Silby said McGuire told him he used it to severe animal heads for his animal head wall-mounts. In the first place, since when does McGuire hunt? And if he *did* hunt, isn't the hunter required to field-dress the animal? And if a hunter field-dresses a kill, why not remove the head there, in the *field?*

"The man *is* strange," Taylor said.

"Silby said the device looked like something from the French Revolution."

"Do you think that's what he's using it for, animal head mounts?" Taylor asked.

"I guess so. What other purpose could there be? Are those things legal to own?"

"You're the lawyer; you tell me. McGuire *does* collect antiques," Taylor answered. "But an antique guillotine is pretty much off the charts, even for McGuire. And, don't forget, the police did suspect him of having something to do with those missing children from 2013."

"You don't really suppose he had anything to do with those missing kids, do you?"

"After all the things I've seen while living in Raventon, *nothing* surprises me anymore, Rommy. I mean, just look at you and Bobbie."

"Touche."

"So, what do you think, Rommy.

"What I think is that tomorrow evening, I'm going to check out this alleged guillotine. Are you at Miss Peasy's?"

"Yes. And you need to get over here now. Remember the dazed man we tried to feed at the Whippoorwill the other night?"

"Of course. Has he been there?"

"Just you get over here. There's more. McGuire's here, too, at Miss Peasy's. He's hanging around the front porch, and he's *not* happy. And, believe me, the plot is *thickening*."

"How so? And what's McGuire doing there?"

"Just get over here."

"On my way."

"Wait, Rommy. The guillotine, tomorrow evening? How are you going to check it out? Knock on his door and waltz on in, saying 'Hello, Mr. McGuire, I'm here to check out your guillotine'. Yeah, that'll work."

"No, Taylor, you forget that I grew up in this town, and I used to play in McGuire's backyard, even ate his figs and dug worms for fishing. He's got a couple of ground-level basement windows back there, and I know how to get to them without being noticed. If those windows are still like they were fifteen years ago, they are unlocked and easy to access without his hearing me. The man's practically deaf, anyway."

"Rommy, that sounds *very* risky. Are you sure you want to do this? By the way, can I come, too?"

"Ha! I knew you couldn't resist a risky mystery, Tay! Of course, you can come."

"What if we find … well, you know … remains."

"*Remains*?"

"The missing kids."

"Seriously?"

"The thought occurs to me."

"Yeah, it *would*. Ever heard of *9-1-1? That's* who we're gonna call."

32

Just as McGuire was leaving Miss Peasy's, Rommy approached the porch and noticed McGuire too late to avoid physical contact. Only the contact was not physical. Rommy winced, unable to avoid certain collision. But McGuire passed through Rommy as if he were not there. Stunned, Rommy continued inside.

"Did … Did you *see* that?"

Sterling followed Taylor outside.

"Saw it, Rommy," Taylor said. "*Now* I'm convinced."

"Convinced of what?" Rommy asked.

"Sterling, what did McGuire mean by 'full resurrection'?"

"Did you say ... *Sterling?*" Rommy asked.

"I can't *tell* you," Taylor said. "I can only *show* you. And open your mind."

"Just that his resurrection into this physical world is not permanent," Sterling answered. "McGuire has his mission, and I mine. We exist on opposite ends of the moral spectrum. McGuire has been allowed one last chance to ... well, make good of his life's gifts. So far, he has failed miserably, and he knows it. He can only delay his eternal fate, not alter it. Thus his pursuit of the Neal watch. And time is of the essence, to us both."

"The watch ... And, if *he* has the watch and fulfills his mission *first*, you ...", Taylor said.

"I will not be allowed to fulfill mine," Sterling finished. "Evil will have won this round."

"May I see the watch?" Taylor asked.

"Yes," Sterling said, handing it to her. Taylor opened its lid.

"So gorgeous!" Taylor exclaimed. "What's this? An inscribed Bible verse, Isaiah 48:9."

"The same verse--" Miss Peasy said.

"Where the bullet stopped," Rommy finished.

"*Specimens,* Rommy. McGuire's *mission*! I know now what McGuire's been up to all these years. We *have* to investigate this guillotine thing Silby told us about." She handed the watch back to Sterling.

"No," Sterling said. "Keep it. You need it more than I right now. If I don't possess it, then neither can McGuire."

Taylor wrapped her fingers around it. "I'll give it back, soon."

"Tomorrow night, then," Rommy said. "Meet me on the sidewalk across from McGuire's house at ten o'clock. There's no moon, plenty of darkness.

"Sounds good." Taylor turned. "Let's get back to Miss Peasy and Sterling. I'll introduce you. You're *not* going to believe this."

"I already *don't*."

"Oh, Rommy," Taylor said, smiling, nudging him in his side, "sometimes one has to give reality a rest!"

33

Rommy sipped his cup of streaming Earl Grey.

"Do you really expect us to believe what you are telling us, Sterling?" Rommy asked. "I mean, you don't look a day over *thirty*. How can we be *certain*, beyond *all* reasonable doubt, that you are who you say you are? Maybe you slipped into Miss Peasy's house, opened the letter box and rifled through them all, familiarizing yourself with the history contained therein."

"He couldn't have," Miss Peasy said.

"And why not?" Rommy asked.

"I understand your doubts, Rommy," Sterling said. "I suppose you'll just have to have faith that I am telling the truth."

"I need more."

"Rommy, you just *witnessed* more, outside there!" Taylor said, pointing toward the front door.

"He couldn't have," Miss Peasy said, "because I keep the box's key on my person at all times, Rommy. It would have taken considerable tampering -- or divine intervention -- to jimmy this box's lock. Do you see any signs of tampering?"

"Miss Peasy, could you hand me the stack of letters?" Sterling asked, pointing to the box.

"No!" Rommy said. "Retrieve them yourself."

"He's studying to be a lawyer, Sterling," Taylor informed.

Sterling sighed. "Very well. But it might be more convincing to you if I just tell you the location of the letter in the box relative to all the other letters."

"What do you mean, Sterling?" Taylor asked.

"The letter to which I refer is the seventeenth letter down from the top of the stack."

Miss Peasy, Rommy, and Taylor stared at the wooden box of letters, not certain who should be the one to confirm Sterling's claim.

"Go ahead, Rommy. You are the greatest of doubters here. It's where I said it is. See for yourself."

Rommy hesitantly went to his knees and counted the letters from the top of the stack.

"One, two, three, four, five, six, seven, eight, nine, ten, eleven … wow, these letters are really *old* … let's see, where was I?"

"Eleven," Taylor said.

"Oh, yes, eleven. Twelve, thirteen, fourteen, fifteen, sixteen … seventeen." Rommy lifted the letter from the box. "Looks like all the others, Vice," Rommy said. "What distinguishes *this* letter as *the* letter?"

"All the envelopes of all the other letters," Sterling noted, "are open. This one is sealed. This letter has never been opened."

"Why?" Miss Peasy asked.

"Because this letter is a hand-copied version of the original letter, number twenty-three in the stack there -- count on, you'll see -- and the envelope of *this* copied version in *not* in my handwriting. I did address the original letter's envelope myself, signed the letter, too, though I did not write the letter. This sealed copy was hand-delivered to Henry's mother *after* the war, along with the original, by the nurse who wrote it for me. She wanted to be sure my family received the letter, even if delivery had to wait until after the war's end, unsure during 1863 how wartime delivery of letters south would survive in hostile territory."

Rommy counted to the twenty-third letter in the stack and removed an unsealed letter. He turned from view of the others and compared the envelope to the unsealed envelope. Rommy took out his pen and some scrap paper from his pocket.

"Here, Mr. Vice," he said. "Write your name as it appears on the original letter, and write the address as it appears on this *un*sealed envelope. There is also something else written on the envelope's back. Write that as well."

"You are a hard nut to crack, Rommy," Sterling said, "but, yes, I will do that."

Sterling took the pen and paper. "So *this* is a twenty-first century pen. Interesting." He wrote. He handed the paper and pen to Taylor. "Please compare the envelope with this paper, Taylor, and then please read the original letter aloud."

Taylor took Sterling's writing and compared it with the unsealed envelope. Rommy peeked over her shoulder. Every letter of Sterling's name, every letter's curve, every curl, every nuance of the handwriting, *all* were identical to that on the unsealed envelope and original letter.

"July 4, 1863," Taylor said. "It's the same date as written on the back of the unsealed envelope." She handed the letters to Rommy. "What else do you need?"

"Why is the sealed letter still sealed?" Miss Peasy asked. "Wouldn't she have wanted to read it?"

"She didn't have to. Not if the letter was hand-delivered from the nurse who transcribed it. Its seal was her way of preserving it unstained and intact, at least in her mind, the most precious letter Sterling -- *I* -- ever wrote, his – *my* -- *last* letter. Besides, she already had the original. Can you read this, Taylor?" Sterling asked as he held out his hand to take the original letter from Rommy.

In stunned, silent amazement, Rommy extended his hand holding the original letter. Taylor took it, carefully opening its creases. She cleared her throat and began to read.

"'July 4, 1863.'" Taylor paused, taking in the incredulity of it all and sighed, holding back her tears. Swallowing, she continued.

"'My Dearest Elizabeth,

"'I have participated in a battle that defies human description, and I have survived it. My survival in its aftermath remains in question. A nurse is taking to paper my dictated words, and I am eternally grateful to her for this service.

"'I was wounded on the third day of this battle in the fields of Gettysburg, Pennsylvania (not far north of the Maryland border) when my rifle was shattered by enemy bullets, sending shards of the barrel's metal, the bullets, too, I was told, into my left breast, shoulder and left arm. I was taken prisoner by Union soldiers and into the care of a Union field hospital, where I now rest after treatment of my wounds. I am told my wounds are infected and gangrenous. A doctor McGuire has changed the dressings of my wounds but refuses to treat them further, all but assuring my death. Maybe shoulder gangrene is simply too difficult to amputate.

"'Even as the nurse writes this, I can feel the throbbing pulse of the infections and the intense pain they cause. I am given some whiskey, but its effects are minimal. I am told by doctor McGuire that I may leave tomorrow a paroled soldier to walk home to Raventon, home to you and the children. I live for that moment, but my body grows weaker by the minute, and it is unlikely I could survive such a walk.

"'Let me tell you about Henry, which I pray you will share with his mother, assuming she does not know. First, let me mention that my life was spared twice during the terrible infantry charge on the battle's third day. I believe you remember the 12-year-old orphaned boy who accompanied me to Virginia to join up with Lee's Army of Northern

Virginia. His name was Charlie Dyer, and he wanted to be a drummer for Robert E. Lee, Marse Robert, he called him. And so he was, tapping out the finest cadences of march any man had ever heard, never halting in the face of imminent danger and death. Courage beyond his years. During the battle's climactic charge, Charlie gave his body as my shield from the bullets of at least two enemy rifles. He was killed falling against me.

"'Charlie carried with him a gold-plated, double-lidded pocket watch, etched with the Old Testament verse, Isaiah 48:9, and a sailing ship. On the watch's face was scribed the name John O. Neal, a Pennsylvania evangelist and divine healer. Unfortunately, doctor McGuire has come into possession of this watch, which he claims in the name of the spoils of war. I call it thievery.

"'As for Henry, he was every bit as sacrificial. Henry tried to protect me from an artillery piece filled with canister, aimed at a group of Confederates of which I was a part, as we stormed a breach in the Union lines at our objective. I saw Henry running toward me, away from the Union line of infantry and guns. Just as the artilleryman pulled the lanyard for discharge, Henry pushed me to the ground. He absorbed countless balls of canister which tore his body to shreds. Those balls were meant for me. Henry Iverson was a hero that day, serving his country as best he knew how, and protecting his comrades until his dying moment.

"'My sweet Elizabeth, I pray to return to you in the coming weeks as my health returns to me, God willing. Please tell the children I love them.

"'Your Loving Sterling.'"

34

Saturday afternoon,
July 5, 2020
3:30PM

McGuire returned from Miss Peasy's home, from his encounter with Sterling Vice. The watch, that treasured spoil of war, he vowed, would once again be his. Without it, his existence would fade into the darkness of his eternity, his allotted time exhausted. His soul would dissolve into the abyss, as if he had never existed.

But he hadn't much time to reclaim it. His window was closing. Soon, his post-mortal journey in the physical realm, as for Sterling as well, would end. McGuire needed to possess the watch of Joseph

O. Neal, for only the watch would buy him more time, and then only if God allowed.

Travis "Digger" McGuire, gifted Civil War surgeon and contemporary preacher, had abused both gifts, selfishly regurgitating contortions of God's Word, while consuming young lives for his own glory and profit.

"Who could be knocking on my door this time of night!" McGuire said. He opened the door.

"Yes, yes, *what!*" he growled.

"Good evening, Mr. McGuire. Please forgive intrusion at such late hour. Allow me to introduce myself," he said, his English broken and his East European accent thick. "My name is Dravik Kryzinkov. This is Vladimir Provich, my trusted and able associate. We represent joint Russian/ American organization working in conjunction with Organs for Lives, an American-based charitable group channeling donated human organs to points abroad as well as to most serious, time-sensitive domestic cases."

"And you want a donation," McGuire interrupted. "Of *money*, that is."

"No, no, please, let me finish. We help facilitate meeting urgent need for such. We noticed your spacious house and believe it to be ... most beneficial to accommodating our base-to-delivery-point requirements for this area of country."

"*My* house? A *base* point for *organ* deliveries?"

"Processing of orders and their deliveries, yes."

"I thought hospitals handled those details."

"Yes, they do, in most instances. Sometimes third party needed, to insure most timely delivery."

"And you want my house for a base," McGuire said.

"*The* base, yes, Mr. McGuire. Allow my entry and I shall explain."

"I don't know, Mr. ... uh, what'd you say your name was?"

"Kryzinkov. But call me Dravik. There is much *financial gain* for you, Mr. McGuire, just for use of your house for maybe a month, perhaps longer."

"*Financial* gain, you say?"

"Indeed. You will be handsomely paid, for your house and for your trouble, I promise you. Entry, please?"

"I -- I suppose there's no harm in that … Dravik." McGuire gave the matter a half-minute's pause. "Maybe you can help me get my pocket watch back. Sure, why not?"

"See, you already get name right. We are off to good start, no?"

35

But, *my* house?"

"Why *not* your house, Mr. McGuire? There are many large, old houses in this neighborhood, but we choose yours. Luck of draw, no? We choose Raventon because it is central point in Birmingham-Chattanooga-Atlanta transportation triangle. Plus, it is central point of superb medical region."

"Okay … I guess. Sounds good enough," McGuire said. "Want me to show you around?"

"Please, my friend, especially basement area."

"Basement area?"

"For office cubicles, out of way of core business."

"Yes, of course. So … how much … financial gain … are we talking here, Mr. Dravik?"

"No 'mister'. Is too formal, and besides, Dravik is first name."

"Of course. My apologies."

"Not at all. Mind if I have drink first?

"Of course, yes. Pardon my lack of manners. What would you like?"

"I have choice?"

"If you choose between milk, water, or orange juice."

"I take orange juice. Have flask of rum here."

"So I see. Okay, orange juice it is. Be right back."

Dravik put his briefcase on the coffee table and opened it. He gazed at the high ceilings and open spaces.

"Is perfect," he whispered. Vladimir nodded agreement.

"Here you go," McGuire said, handing Dravik a glass of orange juice.

"Thank you, my friend." Dravik poured two splashes of rum into the juice. "Make it three," Dravik said with a smile.

"Now, sir," McGuire asked, "how much financial gain are we talking here?"

"Considerable. Tens of thousands, perhaps. Depends."

"U. S. dollars, none of that Confederate junk."

"But of course! We talk details later. First, join me in toast to you, Mr. McGuire, and to our new partnership in delivering needed organs to desperate patients."

McGuire poured himself a glass of milk. The two men touched glasses and drank.

"Now, let me see," Dravik said, reaching into his briefcase.

"What ... what do you have there in that case, Dravik, a contract?" McGuire asked, sipping milk and wiping the sudden blur from his eyes.

"Details later, remember?"

"Looks ... looks like one of my black broad-brimmed Amish hats ... and a frizzy ... white beard ... what's ... what's going on here?"

"It is that, indeed, Mr. McGuire. Tell me how I look wearing them." Dravik donned the hat and beard. "So, then, Travis McGuire, how do you feel?"

"How do I … how do I … *what?*"

"Just as I had hoped. A perfect likeness," Dravik said, glancing at the wall mirror. "And my accent is now less Russian and more American, wouldn't you agree?"

His head spinning, McGuire slumped onto the couch, his countenance not quite as immortal as he had believed. His time … was up.

"Your house is *too* easy to enter, Mr. McGuire, which is how we were able to drug your milk. My country and I thank you for the use of your lovely, large home, but you are no longer welcome in it, nor will you need it."

McGuire tried saying something. Only nothing came out, except his breath of semi-consciousness.

"Very good, Mr. McGuire," Dravik said, checking McGuire's weakening pulse. "You are *most* cooperative."

Two men entered the den from the basement.

"Take him downstairs," Dravik instructed. "Remove his heart, his liver, his kidneys, and his retinas. Do it carefully, but do it fast. Make sure the organs are placed in Sherpa Paks and that the temperature of each is set--and remains--between four degrees Celsius and eight degrees Celsius. Higher or lower, and his organs will die.

"Dispose of the body so that it is never found, not by police, not by cadaver hounds, not by archaeologists a thousand years from now. Not by *anyone, ever*. Do you understand?"

"We understand, sir."

"Very good. Vladimir, you are in charge. Do you remember how to remove the organs properly?"

"Should be no problem, Dravik," Vladimir replied. "I never forget how. Only problem is ... well, I have no anesthesia."

"So ... if McGuire comes to during the harvesting ..." Dravik said, his eyes alight at the possibility.

"I hope for his sake he does not," Vladimir said.

"No matter. He will not live long enough to notice. Bring Sherpa Pak with the organs to me. I must get these organs to drop-off point this evening. Then, we must prepare guillotine. We have many orders for bones."

"Yes, sir," one of the men replied.

They lifted the limp McGuire's body and hauled him down to the basement. Vladimir followed them.

"Now to hire another boy to take package of organs to drop-off point. Must not be late," Dravik said, slipping back into his native Russian accent as he secured to his scalp and forehead the white-frizzed wig and black-nylon brow.

He spent another sixty minutes applying makeup and skin-wrinkling effects, skillfully transforming into McGuire's age, McGuire's likeness. Lastly, he donned McGuire's black, broad-brimmed Amish hat, one of three McGuire owned, a black duster and torn jeans.

"Perfect. Oops," he said, smiling, picking up McGuire's Bible from a table, "must not forget this opiate of the masses."

36

Saturday evening,
July 5, 2020
6:37PM

Silby walked up the squeaky porch steps, as if walking up the steps of the gallows, step by fearful step. He wanted his payment, his hundred dollars, but he did not want to reveal what he had done delivering the bag.

The air reeked of decay. Silby wasn't sure if the odor came from within the house itself or was the wafting of pungent humid stillness, the result of several daily roadkills of squirrels and chipmunks that specked the neighborhood streets nearby. He placed his hand over his nose and mouth. He knocked with three rapid taps on the door, as instructed.

Silby set the heavy black medical bag on the porch planks. He leaned and glanced through a window. No sign of light. Perhaps no one was home. Concluding exactly that, he turned to make his way down those gallows-like porch steps. As he did, the doorknob rattled with movement and the door moaned open. Silby slowly turned.

The 'old man' stood, his frame tall, eyes unblinking and ablaze with the reflections of porch light, the breeze sweeping his white frizz along a horizontal wave across his face.

"You're *late*," Dravik grumbled, adjusting the black hat and taking the medical bag from the boy. "Follow me."

"I'm sorry, sir. Y-you can just pay me right *here*, sir," Silby said, hand extended, a forced smile peeking. "That is, you don't *need* to pay me."

Dravik, with a scowl of objection, turned toward Silby. "You will *follow me*, young man, just as you promised. That, or no payment."

"Yes, sir," Silby replied as he stepped through the half-opened front door, the acrid odor of rotting flesh giving him an unwelcomed smack to his senses. Silby pressed his hand over his nose and mouth, resisting the impulse to vomit. Dravik walked ahead, unmindful of Silby's reaction. "I—I *really* need to get home, sir. I want some mashed potatoes and gravy, some roast..."

"Silence! You will *get* your beef and potatoes, at least your just desserts!"

"My ... *what* desserts?"

"I said silence!"

"Yer, sir."

"So, boy, now that you have had the chance to see my device up close, to give it the cleaning it needed, what do you think?"

"Well, sir, I ... what I mean is ... well, it was quite a mess. Took me a while to get all that blood off it, especially off the wood. What ... what did that blood belong to, anyway?" Silby asked, not wanting to assign the pronoun of 'who'. "That is, what *animal*?"

"Animal mounts, of course. Deer, perhaps? I forget. So many of them, you know. Come down here, boy," the old man said, pointing to the basement door with his skull-handled cane. I want to *praise* you for what cleaning you did so well. And point out what needs *improving*, for next time. The man pulled open the basement door and motioned Silby ahead of him.

"Take a seat, by the device," Dravik said. "Surely you are thirsty, all that pedaling around in the humid evening."

"Yes, sir, a bit thirsty, all right," the boy said through another forced smile.

"Well, then, take this," Dravik said as he offered the boy a glass of cold milk.

"Thank you, sir. Don't mind if I do."

Silby took the glass and drank the milk in one tipping and a few gulps. The man grinned slightly. Silby wiped his mouth clean and thanked him.

"Now then, the device is indeed spotless. An *excellent* job of cleaning, my boy. Excellent, indeed.

Floor, too. Mustn't have the messiness of blood in our midst."

"No, sir," the boy answered, his eyes blinking with heaviness. "The smell's pretty bad, though."

"Yes, we have to work on that. Let's now discuss what needs *improving*, shall we? This medical bag, for instance. It's empty, as it should be." Dravik leaned closer to Silby's ear. "But for the *wrong* reason."

37

The boy's eyes widened, realizing the man knew what had happened.

"It - it was a … an *accident*, sir, truly it *was*." Silby rubbed his eyes.

"I'm sure it was, my boy. I'm sure it was."

Dravik sat in a chair at a round table. He sighed.

"You … you don't have to pay me, sir."

"Agreed," said Dravik. "But you see, your … *accident* … has cost me a *hundred thousand dollars.* Did you *hear* me? I have a client in Moscow waiting for a heart, more accurately, waiting to *pay* for that heart. Spilling that bag's contents -- human organs -- on the sidewalk was a very careless, *costly* mistake indeed, and now I simply must recover that loss. I have no other choice. You understand, I'm sure."

"Human ... But, how ..."

Silby's head spun with dizziness as he collapsed onto the sofa, his arms and legs paralyzed, unable to function. He had just enough cognizance to realize he had been drugged.

Dravik waited a few minutes to ensure total unconsciousness before lifting the boy and placing him on his back, face up, on the slab. He secured the straps around his body, legs, and arms. He lifted the lunette and placed the boy's neck firmly within its hold.

"Vladimir!" Dravik called.

Dravik had hired the boy off the street earlier in the late morning, from the concealment of the house, thus not giving him the opportunity to inform his family or friends of his temporary employment nor to give others a chance to witness the transaction. It was a now-or-never opportunity for the boy, a quick hundred dollars to mop up some blood and to deliver something in a black medical bag. Lunch could wait, the boy had thought. Indeed, it waited. After all, video games were at stake.

Now, no one knew the boy was here, strapped to the slab of the guillotine he had cleaned, about to have his body harvested of its organs for sale to black-market parties worldwide.

"Wha—what are you doing to me?" Silby asked, regaining some of his consciousness, pulling on the straps. "Why am I tied …?"

He looked up and saw the glare from the huge steel blade, the blade he had earlier cleansed of its blood. He tried lifting his head but could not.

"Let me go!" he shouted. "What are you *doing?"*

"Suffer the little children, and forbid them not, to come unto me; for of such is the kingdom of heaven. Matthew nineteen, verse fourteen," said Dravik.

"What? Preacher McGuire, are you *crazy?* You *are* crazy! Just … like they said!"

"SSSHHHH!" said Dravik. "It will be over soon. You will not feel a thing, and you will be with your God. 'For I reckon that the sufferings of this present time are not worthy to be compared with the glory which shall be revealed in us,' sayeth the Lord. Romans eight, verse eighteen. Think of the *glory* into which you are about to enter, boy."

"What accent is that you are speaking with?" Silby asked, detecting a foreign dialect in the words. "Is it tongues? Who *are* you? Are you … really Preacher McGuire? What are you *doing* to me? I've got to get home … get home for supper. Mashed po … tatoes. Let me … go …"

Silby struggled feebly to free himself as he grew weaker from the drug, but he could make no headway against the tightened leather straps. Dravik rested his hand on the blade trigger.

"Wait! Don't! You're – you're *not* Preacher McGuire!" Silby shouted. "I can tell now. Preacher McGuire's eyebrow doesn't … fall … off, like yours … just did."

Dravik touched his forehead. He hadn't noticed. He shrugged.

"Where's *Preacher McGuire? No-o-o-o!"*

"Besides, you owe me *hundred thousand dollars,"* Dravik said, his accent thick, his black hat tipping.

"This is price for your carelessness. Not to mention your young heart and other most profitable organs. Very much appreciated."

Dravik smiled and pressed down on the trigger, releasing the heavy blade. "You feel nothing, I assure you."

SSSHHHHHEEEEWWWWW … THUNK.

38

Matthew 7:15 -- *"Beware of false prophets, which come to you in sheep's clothing, but inwardly they are ravening wolves."*

Monday,
July 7, 2020
8:37PM

Taylor approached the old house. Solving mysteries was her passion, but the guillotine aspect of this mystery deepened her trepidation. "Who owns *guillotines* except the French?" she had earlier asked Rommy.

Still, the intrigue drew her like a magnet. The late evening air drifted like swamp ooze in its slow dance of humidity-fueled fog. The McGuire house sat poised on the hilltop like a vulture on its perch.

"Or, serial killers," she whispered.

Rommy had said to meet him here, across the street beside this oak. Bobbie would try to make it, if she could lift herself from her own fog of flu, which had set in with a vengeance the night before. Taylor had no expectations for seeing Bobbie.

Taylor stared at the house through the grainy dull of dusk, a breeze occasionally tossing strands of hair across her eyes.

"Where *is* Rommy," she whispered, her frustration growing.

Could it be Preacher McGuire is indeed tangled up in the rumors swirling in the undercurrent of Raventon's gossip scene? And if there is a guillotine, like Silby said, what does it mean? Taylor thought.

Taylor Smart had clipped and studied Raventon newspaper articles written over the past few years concerning the missing children, teens mainly, some of whom last had been seen entering Preacher

McGuire's old house around the times of their disappearances.

And *what a house!* The venerable structure peered over the hilltop like a prototype for all haunted houses. Rising full moons took foreboding paths directly over the roofline's center point, a detail not lost on the house's builder.

Dead trees, their limbs bent with the painful twists of time, populated the landscape around the house. Such trees, such yards as this, were frequent Halloween toilet paper targets, limbs clothed to excess with the ghostly streams, despite – *because* of -- Preacher McGuire's helpless, shouted anger directed toward his tormentors.

Investigators had questioned McGuire on several occasions since October of 2013, even executing warrants to search the house. No evidence pointing to malfeasance was found, despite the rumors. The case had gone cold as to the McGuire investigation, its attention grabbed by other tips pointing to unrelated suspects whose wells, likewise, had come up dust-dry. Miss Peasy was prime among those suspects and remained such.

Taylor, of course, was not convinced. Bolstered by McGuire's fiery street preaching a couple of evenings before, by his constant references to how integral suffering was to the maturity of a Christian, to how everyone must die once, Taylor felt the clingy presence of something sinister on these premises. His words, like icy warnings, sent chills over her body.

Taylor glanced at her watch.

C'mon, Rommy! she thought. "I'm early, yes, but you need to be *earlier*. That's what you *do!*"

She wondered if McGuire was in the house or had left for the evening. If she could find a way, a route, into the house, to search it undetected, to find such evidence her instincts nudged her to believe existed, especially to confirm Silby's claim of the guillotine's existence, she was eager to discover it, to exploit it, with or without Rommy.

Rumors, like humor, were anchored in kernels of truth, and Taylor was determined to uncover those kernels, reveal that truth. Unsolved mysteries, after all, demanded such unrelenting determination.

Why Taylor had not noticed this old house before baffled her as she approached the ominous structure. The streets, marked by puddles of rainwater from an afternoon thunderstorm, were quiet, as most residents were captives to their TVs, watching crucial mid-season pennant races or another gripping PBS miniseries.

The fog pressed Taylor's face. Only the opaque flickers from half-working street corner lamps and the soft glows of a few porch lights offered any hint of civilization. A swiftly moving patch of fogless air passed over the trees, revealing evidence of stars that dotted the black night canvas like spilled sugar.

The house certainly *commanded* one's notice. Maybe it was the weed-flanked, dirt driveway that had deflected her attention through the years. Maybe Bobbie had never mentioned the house, which, of course, she *had* mentioned, since Bobbie left no spooky house nor speck of a good mystery *un*mentioned. Maybe its mildewed charcoal-gray façade reminded her of a cave she had just as soon forget.

The house loomed tall, much like Taylor's refurbished house, and probably older. In fact, Mike had once set his sights on this house, in lieu of the house Taylor had moved into when she and her mom moved to Raventon, but it had never been offered for sale. The town's streets were lined with such antebellum structures as this, but *this* ... well, *this* house had its own unique aura of dread surrounding it, like that spider everyone knows lurks somewhere in the room, an aura like no other antebellum house in Raventon.

Its attic dormers protruded like bludgeoned eyes, the breezes softly slapping their shutters with an annoying cadence of inconsistent rhythm. Boards on the house seemed to moan in the breeze with each tick of the clock, as if they harbored souls unable to find their niche, trapped in some transitional eternity, as if begging to be freed from the nails that held them.

The breeze picked up, slashing mown leaves down empty sidewalks, across lawns, and against the broken clapboards and loose-hinged shutters. Taylor glanced toward the west, the horizon a narrow strip of glowing orange-red scattering its waning light onto purple cirrus clouds.

If what Rommy had told her was true, that McGuire owned an antique guillotine and was not just a former preacher but a night-dweller, a peculiar old man seen routinely leaving the house after dark and vanishing into the shadows of sidewalk oaks, showing up on street corners as he mounted atop his wooden box to preach his distorted gospel to whomever showed up, then vanishing to places unknown, maybe now was the best time to explore any truth to the rumors, the gossip, to confirm some of the tales, to find the evidence perhaps heretofore missed by investigators. Rommy said a lot of fantastic things, many of which still were products of his prodigious imagination. Perhaps this was nothing more than more of that. Maybe he had misunderstood Silby. Maybe it was *Silby's* imagination at work here.

By the way, Taylor thought, *what about Silby? I used to see him riding his bike all over town in the summertime. Didn't notice him a single minute today. I'd chalk it up to coincidence, if I were a believer in coincidence.*

Taylor had not noticed anyone exiting the house. She stopped, leaning against an oak tree.

Maybe McGuire's moved, no longer living here. Doubt that, she thought.

They had seen him preaching just this past Friday. Maybe, in this foggy translucence, Taylor had stopped in front of the wrong house, an abandoned house, and *no one* lived here anymore. Plenty of old homes rested empty in Raventon, their owners long since departed in one way or another. Lots of things can happen in a couple of years away at college, including an altered sense of orientation. The house was shrouded in darkness, as if condemned, not a trace of light coming through its windows.

Just who is this Preacher Travis McGuire -- Crazy Travie -- anyway? Taylor wondered. *The wacky babbler. Down deep, who is this man?*

Preacher McGuire was Raventon's firebrand. He shouted – some would claim he sprayed -- God's Word from the pulpit of Cornerstone Covenant Church once upon a long ago, louder and more convincingly than any of his predecessors, yet he was as calm and reassuring after services as a little girl's granddaddy, especially when within sniffing distance of someone's dinner invitation.

McGuire, for going on better than a year, was the Friday-night occupant of the corner of Second Avenue, sometimes Third, and Broad. He came to his preaching spot dressed in his Johnny Cash black, a guitar he never played hanging from one shoulder and a Civil War military drum hanging from the other, as he waved his tattered Bible like a limp newspaper, and he shouted his seasoned brand of Gospel fire, pontificating his version of the destruction of morality and its requisite punishment of suffering, particularly as such pertained to young people, and how God would not let the sins of malleable youth stand, how God would exact His vengeance, His justice, His justification of suffering, and the end of this world and its manmade, Jesus-denying comforts. He was nothing if not one continuous sentence.

39

Most folks ignored McGuire, writing him off as the product of senility, despite the growl of his voice and the crisp, articulate anger that wrapped its convincing coils around his words. McGuire's white frizzes of hair streamed in the breezes like the ghost of John Brown's. Indeed, Crazy Travie seemed as much a specter as a spectacle.

Taylor unwrapped a stick of gum but held it, nervously fiddling with its pliability, rolling it, unrolling it, twisting it. The orange glow of the setting sun vanished below the distant mountains. A leaf slapped her cheek, startling her. She wiped away the moisture it left.

Taylor was not about to accept at face value such reports, such rumors – tall tales, she believed -- of a *guillotine* inside that house. In *America*, in *these* parts, in *this* century? She had to see it for herself.

Rommy, she remembered from Blythington's game, was prone to exaggeration, if not outright falsehoods, even in immediate word-of-mouth exchanges. Once upon a time, Taylor would have written off rumors such as this as nothing more than attention-grabbing lies, but Rommy was not the Pilfree of old. He was a second-year Pre-Law major, at Harvard, no less. He had crossed the Rubicon -- some might say the Rubik's Cubicon -- into the age of maturity and truth, Taylor believed.

What did *not* sit well in Taylor's mind was not so much the rumors of a guillotine within these spook–flushed, paint-peeling, clapboard-shaking walls, but the coincidental timing of five missing teens over the past *three weeks*, in addition to the unsolved episodes of eight teens gone missing from October 2013 until July of this year. These thirteen teens had disappeared without the slightest of physical traces, with no evidence of wrongdoing, yet the rumors said otherwise. Rumors being rumors, each pointed its finger at the Witch of Raventon. Besides, Taylor did not subscribe to coincidence.

Taylor thought about phoning Bobbie, asking her to join her, but she remembered Bobbie was in bed with the flu. Rommy, of course, might've forgotten his appointment with Taylor and was busy with summer homework, or Rubik's Cubes, or writing draft legislation for the senator for whom he might be interning, or some other mental distraction.

Summer break was supposed to be spent doing nothing, hanging out at the beach, hiking in the mountains, and sleeping late, anything *not requiring* a brain.

The thought of a guillotine, a *working* guillotine, in sleepy Raventon, linked possibly to thirteen missing kids, scooped into Taylor's curious soul like a hot spoon into ice cream. The very thought of the possibility of such a link was disturbing beyond words. This was one rumor worth dispelling. Or confirming.

Taylor heard the muffled sound of a squeaking door. She stood straight up, dropping her twisted gum to the ground. She swirled her arm back and forth through the fog, as if to clear it away. Someone from inside that house was coming out. A silhouetted figure emerged, carrying a cane in one hand and a large bag in the other. Preacher McGuire, indeed, Taylor could see as she squinted through the strèet-lightened fog, his white frizz flowing behind him. The man slowly descended the front porch steps, his black duster whipping his thighs, and ambled toward the sidewalk. Taylor edged behind the thick oak, out of his line of sight.

McGuire blended into the night, like ink on black paper. Taylor waited several more minutes before starting for the old house.

Stepping onto the front porch and craning her neck in the direction McGuire had taken, she pulled her flashlight from her back pocket. She shone the light through one of the glass panels that flanked the door. Nothing unusual, she noted, though the flashlight's glare impeded any clear view.

Instinctively, she grabbed the doorknob and gave it a turn.

Unlocked!

She shrugged off her initial surprise, her reflex to flee the scene, just as temptation wrapped its tentacles around her, opting instead for the opportunity she'd just been handed. Slowly, she pushed the door open and cringed with each growl the door emitted, certain such would reverberate through the neighborhood and reveal her presence. Her heart pounded, knowing she was committing at least half the crime of breaking and entering. She was not there to vandalize or to steal, she rationalized, and thus continued the entering.

Dark is as dark does, and the dark of McGuire's house was no exception. Taylor pointed her flashlight forward and scanned the room, raising and lowering the light. Eerie paintings and portraits hung tilted on the walls. Newspapers lay scattered on the hardwood floors. Juice boxes and crusts of sandwiches dotted the den hardwood. An open Bible rested on a side table next to a recliner. The air smelled of age, like buckets of ancient, unwashed laundry and the pungent remnants of 100-year-old paint.

Taylor's light caught a painting leaning against the wall above the mantle. She stepped closer. The painting, framed in ornate gold, depicted a large crowd gathered in an open space surrounded by Romanesque buildings. In the center of this space was a tall device. Taylor gasped. The device was a guillotine, and the man standing next to the guillotine was holding in his hand the head of its latest victim, blood spilling from the neck.

"Maybe this is what Silby had seen," Taylor whispered.

Next to the painting, against the wall, stood a plaque, the words "Suffer the little children, and forbid them not, to come unto me" burned into the wood.

At least the rumor's half true, Taylor thought. *He does have a painting of a guillotine. Wait, what's this?*

Taylor noticed the unkempt ruffle of a white cloth spread over a round table a few yards away. Moving towards it, she saw this was no cloth. This instead was a stack of papers, architectural-quality drawings of … a *guillotine.*

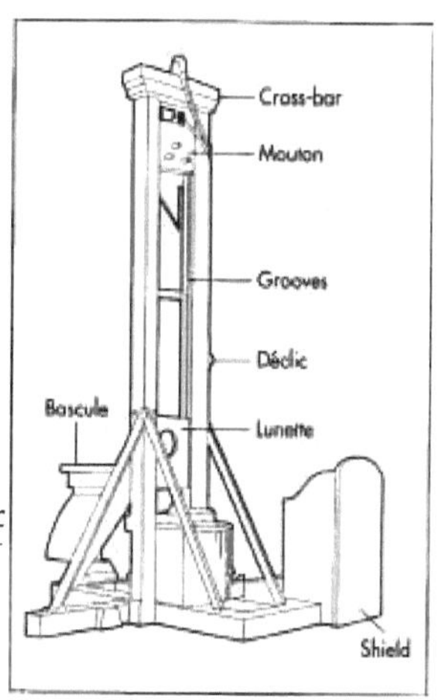

40

Taylor lifted each sheet. "Is McGuire *building* a guillotine?" she whispered. "Maybe Silby was right about this one."

Taylor was startled by the turning of a door's knob and the groan of its opening. She glanced left and right looking for a quick escape or place to hide. She spotted a partially opened door, a cupboard door, she presumed, and made a dash for it. But it wasn't a cupboard door. Opening it, she saw stairs descending into blackness. She had no time to find someplace else. Someone, Crazy Travie perhaps, had entered, clicking the door closed behind. Taylor could hear the shuffling of feet scraping across newspapers and sandwich crusts.

She stepped aboard the top step and pulled the door closed, leaving a sliver of space for the slimmest of views. The shuffling feet drew closer, accompanied by their own bobbing light. Then she could see clearly who this person was.

"Rommy!" Taylor whispered, opening the door.

"AAAAAHHH!!"

Startled, Rommy jumped, facing the opened door.

"Now, *that's* the Rommy I remember. What are *you* doing in here?"

"I could ask the same of *you*, Taylor Smart! And so I will. Taylor Smart, what are *you* doing in here?"

"Exploring this spooky old McGuire house, the very house you told us you wanted to investigate tonight."

"Spooky, indeed," Rommy agreed, surveying the rooms in sight.

"How'd you know McGuire wasn't here, Rommy?"

"Didn't know for sure. House was dark, but I saw someone entering through the front door. I thought it might have been you going inside."

"You could tell it was a *female*, but not McGuire?" Taylor asked. "Through this fog?"

"Well, yeah! I mean, I'm not so much the clueless doofus I was those few years ago. I can tell a female from a male, even in the foggy translucence of darkness."

"Is Bobbie still sick."

"She is - or *was* - but she said she'd try to make it down here tonight if at all possible. I've been doing some exploring of my own, before you got here, even before Crazy Travie left a while ago."

"You were in here while McGuire was still in this house?"

"In the basement, yes."

"Hope she feels like coming," Taylor said.

"Me, too."

"How'd you get in without anyone seeing you, *hearing* you?"

"Snuck in the basement window, 'round back. Remember, McGuire's backyard was once a playground of mine. Besides, he's deaf as an earless possum, anyway. Let me show you what I've found, over here."

"You found something?"

"Over yonder, on that table there," Rommy said, pointing to the same papers Taylor had seen.

Taylor stepped over to the table.

"Strange," Taylor observed with a soft chuckle.

"Strange? What?"

"Hearing you say *'yonder'*, Mr. Harvard law-boy."

"When in Raventon ..."

"Yeah, blueprints of a guillotine," Taylor said. "I saw 'em. And ..."

"There's more," Rommy said.

"Don't tell me ...!"

"Yep. Silby was right. Crazy Travie's got himself a *guillotine,* all right," Rommy said. "More than just mere *blueprints* for one of these puppies."

"I saw these drawings, too, just minutes before you came into the kitchen, Rommy. Scattered pieces of sandwiches, too. Rotwurst and bleu cheese, if I'm not mistaken. No wonder this dump smells like ... well, like a *dump*."

"*No*, Taylor, he's *really* got himself a guillotine. In the *basement*."

"The *basement? That* basement?" Taylor asked as she tilted her head toward the basement door.

"I *saw* it down there, in all its ten-foot, splintered hardwood glory, huge metal blade shimmering like sunlight on a frozen lake. It's got a spoked crank and a ship's rope for hoisting the blade. It's got a plank as long as a body, straps, too, for anyone unlucky enough to become its victim. It's got two semi-circles, lunettes, I think they're called, to fit around the neck, and it's got a basket for … well, you know what for."

"Did you see any …"

"Blood? Didn't really look."

"How could you *not* look? Guillotines aren't *paperweights*."

"Didn't expect any blood, I guess."

"But the *animal head mounts* Silby spoke of …"

"Didn't Silby say McGuire had hired him to *clean* that guillotine of blood?"

"Lawyers. Okay, *show* me said guillotine," Taylor said.

"Follow me."

"What was that?" Taylor asked, turning toward the parlor and the front door.

"Could be ol' man McGuire. Listen."

The front door slowly opened, each groan of the hinges more agonizing than the previous. Feet scraped the floor, and the door was clicked shut.

"C'mon!" Rommy whispered, urging Taylor down the basement steps. Rommy quietly closed the door. The two stepped the thirteen basement stairs as gently as possible and onto the dirt floor.

"Hear anything," Taylor whispered.

Rommy paused, holding his breath. "No, but *somebody's* up there, maybe more than one. We just have to be dead silent."

"More than one? And don't say 'dead'."

"There it is, Taylor Smart," Rommy whispered, shining his flashlight and pointing.

"Wow."

"To say the least."

"How're we getting *out* of here," Taylor asked.

"Basement window, over there," Rommy replied, pointing his flashlight toward the spider-webbed window. "I left it wide open."

Taylor gazed wide-eyed upon the structure, its tall, parallel four-by-eight beams looming skyward, anchored by four forty-five degree planks bolted to a square base. In between the thick beams, ten feet up, was a glistening blade waiting to be dropped.

Taylor knew better than to speak at this moment but did manage an audible gasp.

"Look," Rommy pointed, "it's on casters, for rolling. I think it was rolled from that room."

Both approached one of the side rooms in the semi-finished basement, its 12-foot-tall door partially open. Taylor lifted her flashlight, shining it through the open space.

"It's insulated, padded, like some *asylum* room for the criminally *insane,*" she whispered.

"Wow," Rommy uttered.

"Your legalese fails you, Rommy."

"What I mean is, maybe this padded room is meant not just for storing a guillotine but for muffling screams."

"Man, I bet you're a hoot on dates."

The two stepped into the tall, padded room.

"On the floor. *Look!"* Taylor said. *"Blood. Lots …* of blood. And blood is *all over* the bottom of that guillotine. Looks like Silby missed a spot. I see at least four head mounts on the walls, deer maybe?"

"Could have been used for that, I hope, but Taylor, we've got to get out of here, before McGuire finds us."

"What's *this?"* Taylor asked.

"What's *what, where?"*

"Oh my gosh!" Taylor uttered. "Down *there."*

Rommy followed the flashlight's beam to a corner of the basement, near the tall door. On the dirt floor was a severed human hand.

"Time to exit, stage left, Taylor."

"You *think? Shhh!"*

Taylor heard the basement door pushed open.

"Who is there!"

Taylor and Rommy stood as still as the guillotine near them, a solid twenty feet from the open basement window.

"That voice," Taylor whispered. "Sounds *Russian.*"

"You're discerning accents at a time like this? Let's *go!*"

Both ran toward the window as Dravik stepped down the stairs.

"Who is *there?*"

Dravik saw only the soles of Rommy's shoes as Taylor and Rommy escaped through the window.

"Come back here, you!" he shouted. "Vladimir, go to backyard. Someone's been in basement."

Vladimir ran out the kitchen door but saw nothing through the fog and darkness. A squirrel scampered across his front, and an owl hooted from a distant branch. A siren wailed from a few miles away. Taylor and Rommy crouched low, unseen amid the boxwood fence at the rear of the backyard. They now realized they had stumbled onto something nefarious, terrifying. They held their breath as tightly as the gold of Fort Knox.

41

"We've got to get the police to that house," Taylor whispered.

"I know, I know," Rommy replied. "But what if it's *nothing*?"

"Hey, guys!"

"What? *Bobbie*? How … What are you doing here? I thought you were still feeling rough."

"And I love you, too, Rommy Bojo."

"No, we're *glad* you're here, but I just thought …"

"Yeah, I did, too, but I can't let you guys have *all* the fun, now can I?"

"Keep it *quiet*, you two!" Taylor whispered. "Bobbie, there *is* a guillotine in McGuire's house, in the basement."

"And someone other than McGuire is in there as well," Rommy added.

"Reckon who it is?"

"A human hand is *not* nothing, Rommy," Taylor said.

"What *human* hand?" Bobbie asked.

"Could have been a Halloween prop," Rommy offered.

"Halloween's five months away. And what about that *accent*, Rommy?" Taylor asked. "A *Halloween* accent?"

"Let's go over to Silby's house and see if we can get some additional info on that guillotine," Bobbie suggested. "After all, he *did* say he cleaned it."

"Did a poor job of that cleaning, if you ask me," Taylor replied. "But, yes, let's go talk to Silby. I have a few questions for him."

The three climbed into Rommy's Mustang and made their way to Silby Johnson's house.

Taylor knocked on his front door. Silby's mom answered the knock. She wiped tears away from her eyes.

"H-hello, Mrs. Johnson," Taylor said, sensing their timing was bad. "We … we were wondering if we might … speak with Silby for a few minutes … if we're not interrupting anything, of course."

"You *could*, Taylor … if he were here. He did not come home last evening."

"Didn't … didn't come home, Mrs. Johnson?" Rommy asked.

"Went for a bike ride in the neighborhood yesterday morning. He never came home. Had roast beef and mashed potatoes all ready for him. He *loves* roast beef and mashed potatoes," Mrs. Johnson said through her rising sobs. "*Wild wolves* couldn't tear him away from such a supper."

Rommy looked at Taylor and Bobbie.

"Have you filed a missing-persons report, Mrs. Johnson?" Rommy asked.

She looked at Rommy as her weeping intensified. "Didn't think I *needed* to. Didn't want to even *think* about needing to."

"Call the police, Mrs. Johnson," Taylor said. "They need to know. They'll find him for you."

Taylor, Rommy and Bobbie turned to leave.

"Could ... could you tell the police for me?" she asked.

"Yes, ma'am," Taylor responded, "we could, and we will. Let's go, Rommy."

"Bye, Mrs. Johnson," Bobbie said. "And try not to worry too much. He's okay ... I'm sure of it. We'll be back."

42

Tuesday
July 8, 2020
9:30AM

The Raventon Three told the police about their Saturday encounter with Silby, as well as their knowledge of the guillotine in the McGuire basement.

"Not against the law to *own* a guillotine, you know," Officer Clayton said. "It's what one does *with* a guillotine that makes or breaks its ownership. Speaking of which, you do realize you could be arrested for breaking and entering, don't you, Taylor? You, too, Pilfree," Officer Clayton said.

"Uh … you can call me Rommy, sir."

"Rommy? Since when?"

"Since Harvard, end of freshman year."

"Growing up, are you?"

"Getting there, sir. Sometimes feels like too soon."

"What are you studying, son?"

"Pre-law, sir."

"Well, then, you ought to know better."

"Yes, sir, I do. Haven't quite finished the growing-up part, I suppose, but making quick progress."

"I hear you. I have a son in middle school. Seems like yesterday I was changing his diaper. Anyhoo, back to breaking and entering. There *is* a law against that," Clayton said.

"I committed *no* breaking, officer," Taylor said. "Just the entering, but *please*, you *have* to come check this out. His front door was unlocked, and--."

"What about the hand, officer?" Rommy interrupted.

"As a pre-law student, Rommy," Clayton explained, "you should know that's putting the cart before the horse. You would *not* have seen this alleged hand had you not *first illegally entered*. You had no search warrant."

"Inevitable discovery?" Rommy said, eyebrows raised, knowing better.

"Don't push your luck."

"Understood, officer."

"But, your intentions were good, not criminal, and for that you'll get my break. Just wish you had contacted us before you attempted this. McGuire could have *shot* you for this, and that would *not* have been illegal."

"We're sorry, officer," Taylor said. "Won't happen again."

"See that it doesn't."

"We *did* see a guillotine in Crazy Tra … Preacher McGuire's basement -- must've been as tall as a basketball goal -- *and* a severed hand, a small one," Rommy said, implying the hand might be that of a child's or small teen's.

"I do *not* believe Silby's disappearance is a coincidence," Taylor offered, "and I'm not suggesting the hand is *his*, but ... *For the love of God,* just check it out. If we're wrong, we deserve to be arrested."

"Speak for yourself, Taylor," Bobbie said.

"But if we're right ...".

"She speaks for me as well, Bobbie," Rommy noted.

"Agreed. Check it out, officer," Bobbie echoed. "Please?"

"Let's go, y'all," Officer Clayton said. "I just hope McGuire's home."

"When we escaped through that basement window, *somebody* was there in that house with us, but I don't think it was McGuire," Taylor said.

"Then who?" Clayton asked.

"No way to know. But I've got a bad feeling about McGuire's safety." *Not that his safety matters,* she thought.

"What makes you so sure that what you saw was a severed hand?" Clayton asked. "Maybe it was an animal paw or a Halloween prop, maybe no more than a wadded piece of paper."

"I wish it were *any* of those, sir," Rommy said.

"I must say that it sure *looked* like a hand, fingers and all," Taylor added. "Although we did shine some good light on it, I must also say that we did not get very close to it. And it was dark, and we did not have a lot of time to confirm much of what we think we saw."

"Here's McGuire's house," Clayton said. "You three come with me, but *I'll* do the talking. Do I make myself clear?"

"Crystal, sir," Rommy answered.

43

Officer Clayton knocked on the front door. "Spookiest damn house in Raventon, this old place of McGuire's. You do know that McGuire was suspected for a while in the cases of those missing teens from 2013."

"Yes, I've read about those cases, sir," Taylor said.

"Never found their bodies. Had to assume foul play," Clayton said. "Now five more are missing. Scares the bejesus out of me."

"Make that *six* more, sir," Rommy said in reference to Silby.

"Correction noted, Rommy. Maybe this sixth will turn out to be nothing."

A man pulled open the front door. "How may I help you, officer?" the man asked.

"McGuire home?" Clayton asked.

"In the den, sir. Come in."

"Thank you."

"Who is it, Hughes?"

"A police officer, sir. And three others."

"Police officer?"

"Yes, sir. Officer ..."

"Clayton, Rory Clayton. I have with me Taylor Smart, Bobbie Harwell, and Pil ... I mean, Rommy Bojo. Perhaps you know them?"

"No, sir, I do not."

"Thanks, Hughes. I'll take it from here. Tea, officer?"

"Thanks, no. I'm afraid these three have a confession to make to you, sir."

"Confession? What sort of ... confession?"

"Taylor, you want to take this?"

"Sir ... Mr. McGuire, I ... that is, Rommy and I ... sort of ... well, we entered your house ... last night."

"*Entered* my house?" Dravik said, wearing his McGuire attire, feigning first surprise, then disgust and anger, but satisfied he had learned his intruders. "Why did you come into my house?"

"Well, sir, they tell me that a young lad, thirteen years of age, was hired by you to … clean your … your guillotine."

Dravik spit into Rommy's face a sip of tea he'd just taken, continuing the ruse.

"I guess I deserved that…" Rommy whispered, taking a handkerchief from his pocket and wiping his face.

"Forgive me, please, but a … *Guillotine?* I have *no* such device! And I have hired *no one* to clean *anything* of any sort," shouted Dravik.

"They say you have it in your basement, sir," Officer Clayton said. "Mind if I take a look? Won't take but a minute of your time to put this whole thing to rest."

"Not that I do, because I *don't*, but when did it become unlawful to own a guillotine, anyway," Dravik asked.

"Nothing unlawful about it, sir, but these kids claim they also saw a severed *hand* on your basement floor."

"A *sev*--. This is getting ridiculous, to say the *least*, officer. Have you kids been drinking?"

"I know, Mr. McGuire, but we do have a missing-persons report on the boy, one Silby Johnson. You did hire him to make a delivery for you ...?"

"No. He came by; we chatted. Somehow the conversation drifted to antiques. I offered to give him a black medical bag, from the Civil War. He took it, and then he pedaled home for his lunch of … what was it … oh, yes, roast beef and mashed potatoes."

"Okay. Please understand that I have to follow up on this, on any tips. May we come inside?"

"I understand, officer. Sure, follow me."

Dravik grabbed the skull-capped cane and hobbled toward the basement door in the kitchen.

Rommy leaned and whispered in Taylor's ear, "Where are all the animal head mounts? They're *gone*."

"And he's denied hiring Silby," Taylor replied. "Something's definitely not right here. Silby had that black medical bag when we saw him. Why would he make up some story about a delivery for McGuire? He's the most *honest* kid I know of."

"And what do you suppose, then, was the "delivery" inside that black medical bag?" Rommy asked.

"Y'all coming?" Clayton asked.

"Yes, sir, coming."

The four followed the disguised Dravik down the basement stairs. Dravik flipped the light switch.

The only signs of habitation were the couch, a coffee table, an end table and lamp, a stereo, a dart board, and a framed print of Van Gogh's "Starry Night". On the coffee table were a glass bowl of Hershey kisses, a carafe of burgundy, and three upside-down, unused glasses.

"I … uh … I don't see a guillotine, Rommy," Clayton said.

"It was here. It was … *here,*" Rommy insisted. "That *door!* Open that door there. The guillotine was on wheeled casters. No doubt it's been *rolled* into that room there."

"Mind If I open this door, Mr. McGuire?"

"Not at all, officer. Be my guest."

Officer Clayton pulled open the door.

Taylor gasped. "A *laundry* room?"

"Where are the padded walls?" Rommy asked, touching the walls and shaking the washing machine to make sure it was real.

"Padded walls?" Dravik said, laughing. "Seems you three just might need some padded walls yourselves."

Rommy stepped to the corner where they had seen a severed hand. None existed.

"I ought to arrest you three right here, right now," Officer Clayton said, hand resting on his belted cuffs.

"*Three?* You mean *two*, right?" Bobbie said.

"And you are telling me *unequivocally* you hired no one yesterday to make any delivery for you?" Clayton asked.

"*No!* For what purpose? I hire *no one!*"

"Okay, I *get* it. But, I had to ask," Clayton said.

Taylor leaned in toward Rommy's ear. "There's that *accent* again," she whispered. "I *swear* it's Russian. Is McGuire *Russian*? I thought he was Scottish."

"A *laundry* room?" Rommy whispered, pushing on the walls he was convinced were padded. "Maybe the better question is, is that Russian ... *McGuire?"*

Taylor looked at Rommy and Bobbie, left eyebrow raised, an epiphany lighting a candle over her head.

"Let's go, y'all," Clayton said. "Want me to press charges, Mr. McGuire?"

Dravik sighed. "No," he said after a moment's ponder. "No, let them go. I think they have learned their lesson. Though I do think God intends young people, all people, really, but particularly the young, to suffer to fully earn their salvation, and some suffering here might do them good. But, no. Just take them out of my sight. And make sure they stay away from here."

"You can *count* on that, Mr. McGuire."

"I thought salvation was *free*, Mr. McGuire," Taylor said. "As in, *no charge*."

"Young lady, have you not heard that Paul asked thrice for his thorn to be removed, and God refused, saying, 'My grace is sufficient for thee'?"

"I know it well, sir," Taylor replied. "I also know that suffering is *not* a condition for salvation."

"Enough, Taylor," Clayton said. "Let's go."

"I hope you find missing boy, officer," Dravik said with almost total abandonment of his American accent. Clayton had not noticed.

"Probably nothing to it, Mr. McGuire. Boys will be boys. He probably camped out with friends somewhere. Bet he shows up today. Thank you for your cooperation and hospitality. And your tolerance for our intrusion."

"You are quite welcome; glad to cooperate in any way I can. Just make sure those kids stay away."

"They'll stay away, all right. Ain't that so, Taylor?"

"Yes, sir."

"Have a pleasant day, Mr. McGuire."

Taylor's and Dravik's eyes locked together as the group exited the house.

That sound! He heard it, too. A human voice coming from upstairs. This dude seems taller, less slumped than the McGuire I remember preaching from that portable wooden stoop of his, Taylor thought. *And that accent … a genuine accent, or just an accident? There's something wrong with this picture, and this man knows that I know that.*

As the four were leaving McGuire's house, Taylor stopped. She turned. Her eyes opened wide. She stood as still as a tree, and she listened.

Outside the house and off the McGuire property, Clayton stopped the Raventon Three. He sighed.

"I ought to lock you two up," he said, "really, I should."

"*Finally,* I'm not included in all this talk of crime and punishment," Bobbie said.

"You're *this close* to guilt by association, Bobbie Leigh Harwell," Clayton said.

"It's Bobbie, now, sir," she replied.

"Bobbie?" Clayton asked. "Since when?"

"Since I grew up," she replied.

"Yeah, well, that's a debatable statement. Now, *listen* to me, you three. Keep away from McGuire, from his house, too. And be thankful I'm in a good mood."

"Thank you, Officer Clayton," Taylor said. "We'll be good, we promise. But please hear me on this."

"Hear you on what? *Now* what?" Clayton demanded.

44

"Officer Clayton, I know you doubt our credibility now, and knowing that, I probably should say nothing about what I just heard back there, as we were leaving his parlor."

"What you heard?" Rommy said. "I heard something, too, but I didn't think I should bring it up. Not now, at least. Did we hear the same thing, Taylor?"

"What are you kids talking about *now?*" Clayton asked, his patience growing thin.

"Rommy, if you heard the whimpering voice of a child, then, yes, we heard the same thing."

"What?" Officer Clayton and Bobbie said in unison.

"That's exactly what it was, officer," Taylor said. "The whimpering of a child, a child in *distress*. McGuire -- if that's who that man really is -- noticed it as well. His eyes reacted at the same time I heard it."

Clayton stared lasers at Rommy and Taylor. "Are you freakin *kidding* me?" he said.

"No, sir, we are not," Taylor replied. "Didn't you notice the change in McGuire's accent, Officer Clayton? For a second, he sounded … *Russian*."

"There's something else, too, officer," Rommy said. "I noticed this when we were in the house last night, Taylor. Remember the guillotine drawings? There was a name printed in the bottom-right corner of that drawing."

"A name?" Taylor asked. "Whose?"

"A … Dravik something … *Kryzinkov.*"

"Sounds *Russian* to me!" Bobbie said.

Clayton said nothing for a few long seconds. That name rang a bell.

"Dravik Kryzinkov ... is number *one* on the FBI's most-wanted. He traffics human organs."

"Oh my *Lord*!" Taylor exclaimed.

"You know what, I believe you heard what you heard. I believe Silby's in there. In fact, I *know* he is. Dead or alive, is the question. You kids might frustrate the Dickens out of me, but you have stumbled onto something huge. I'm calling for backup. You kids get in your car and drive off, but park a couple of streets down, maybe East third Street. I'll do the same. Stay out of sight! And out of the way. Got to play this one cool."

"Yes, sir," Taylor said. "Let's go, guys!"

Clayton drove away. The Raventon Three watched as his car rounded the curve.

"Okay, what's the plan?" Rommy asked, in no way willing to leave the plan in the hands of mere backup.

"Did you not hear the man?" Bobbie asked.

"I'm with Rommy," Taylor said quietly, eyes fixed upon the gray McGuire house. "That was *not* McGuire. That was Dravik himself. I'm betting Silby's in that house, and we have *no* time to waste.

Rommy, do you think that basement window is still available?"

"Probably not, but it's worth a look."

"Are you *crazy?*" Bobbie said, clearly frustrated. "You must be *dreaming!*"

"There's a kid missing," said Rommy. "I know Silby Johnson well, and I know he's not a liar. I *do* believe he was in the process of making a delivery for McGuire - or for whoever is *posing* as McGuire. And Taylor and I are not liars, either. We *saw* that guillotine. We *saw* those animal head mounts. We *saw* all the blood. We *saw* the severed hand. This is *no* dream. But it just *might* be a nightmare. We have to get to the bottom of this, Bobbie."

"So, what do you propose we *do?*" Bobbie asked. "McGuire will have us arrested if we're caught on his property, let alone inside his house. You can kiss your Harvard law degree and career goodbye if that happens."

"Have faith, Bobbie," Taylor said. "That's *not* McGuire. Officer Clayton knows that, too. Only one who'll be arrested is … that man."

"I know, I know. We've been through a lot, we Raventon Three," Bobbie affirmed. "We'll get through this, too. Guess I just miss the good ol' days of mindless holiday fun."

"Me, too," Taylor said, her hand on Bobbie's shoulder. "So, Rommy, what's the plan?"

45

"I asked you first."

"Maybe we should wait--" Bobbie started.

"Bobbie, sweetie, you are going to be my *wife*. Pretend Silby's our kid. Now, what would *you* do?"

"Wait a minute!" Taylor said. "Bobbie, you're marrying ... *'Doofus'*?"

"Time out!" Bobbie said. "Your *wife?* That's your idea of a *proposal?"*

"As a matter of fact, yes ... Yes, it is." Rommy smiled.

"I know it's genuine because only *you* would propose like that. And I *accept*!" Bobbie and Rommy kissed.

"Ah, love," Taylor said with a sigh. "Ain't it *grand!*"

"Yes, and you're my maid of honor. Now let's get moving! Can't plan a wedding with *this* hanging over us!"

"You heard the girl," Rommy said, smiling.

46

"Taylor, are you okay?" Bobbie asked.

"Fine ... I think. Felt some fluttering in here for a few seconds," Taylor said, tapping her chest. "Got a bit dizzy, but I'm ... I'm fine now, I think."

"How long has it been?" Rommy asked.

"The heart? Four years, almost. Dr. Smith said I'd have moments like this. Nothing to worry about, he said. Hope he's right."

"Did you ever learn who your heart's original owner was?" Rommy asked.

"Now that I think about it, no. I was told the source was "local", whatever that means. Just thankful to get it."

"I see you've got that Blythington red ribbon around your wrist," Bobbie said.

"A bit of luck never hurts," Taylor said.

"Sure doesn't. Did you say yours is a ... *local* heart?" Rommy asked.

"That's what I was told by Doctor ... wait ... You don't think ...".

"No, I don't think so, Taylor, and neither should you," Rommy said. "I mean, what are the chances ...?"

Taylor felt the fluttering again, this time for a bit longer and more pronounced. She took a few deep breaths.

"So, you two ready for this?" Rommy asked.

"Ready and willing, Rommy," Taylor said, sighing. "Take us to that beloved backyard of your childhood memories, to that basement window that surely by now has not only been locked but barricaded. Have you noticed any activity around the house in the past couple of days?"

"Haven't been close enough to it since Sunday to notice," Rommy said. "And, yes, I do expect we'll encounter some resistance at that window. But we do have an alternative."

"An alternative?" Bobbie asked.

"Plan B. The storm shelter. Leads straight down to the basement. McGuire never locked that thing, and I'm counting on his imposter to continue the ignorance of it."

"Everybody mute your phones," Taylor said.

"Got a Plan C?" Bobbie asked.

The Raventon Three crossed Watson and headed up Third Street, passing antebellum home after antebellum home, the sparkling grandeur of these structures a tourism magnet. The sky hung clear, except for some storms bubbling to the west.

47

"Officer Clayton and his backup will be here soon," Rommy said. "We've got to act before they flush the covey. There's the storm shelter."

"Flush the covey?" Bobbie whispered.

A tall, unclipped row of boxwood shrubs obscured any clear line of sight from the house to the backyard. Rommy scampered low to the ground to the shelter's door and paused. He pulled on the door handle, lifting it open. He motioned for Taylor and Bobbie.

"Does this shelter connect to the basement?" Taylor asked.

"Once upon a time it did. Let's hope it still does."

"Shhhh! I hear something."

"Me, too," Rommy said. "The whimpering voice of a child."

"He's in there," Taylor said. "Through this door!"

"Wait. Do you hear other voices?" Bobbie asked, her ear pressed to the door.

All listened. No one else was heard.

"He's alone?" Taylor said.

"Door's unlocked," Rommy noticed, turning the knob. Gently he pulled the door ajar, enough to get a glimpse of the room's contents.

In the shadowed, dim lighting, the guillotine stood tall, locked and loaded, its shimmering blade high. On the slab lay Silby, his mouth stuffed with a cloth restraint, his body strapped prone on his back, the heavy blade in his full, terrified view, and a white-clothed table of surgical tools beside him.

"Is he--"

"Alive, yes," Rommy answered.

Silby saw the three. His eyes widened with hope.

"Shhhh!" Taylor whispered. "Don't make a sound."

"Where's Dravik?" Rommy asked.

Silby turned his line of sight upward, indicating Dravik was upstairs.

"Come on," Taylor urged. "Now or never!"

The Raventon Three rushed through the door and to Silby's side. Taylor unbuckled the straps and removed the mouth gag.

"*Quiet*!" Taylor said, her finger over her lips.

At that moment, the upstairs basement door opened.

"And now, Silby, your time has come," Dravik said as he walked down the steps. "We make sure this time blade does not get caught and stopped by rope. I assure you that you feel no pain. Your organs are needed by desperate customers, all willing to pay top dollar, and ... *What is this?"*

Dravik, as he stepped from the shadows of the stairs to the low light of the basement, was greeted by a vacant slab, a mouth gag resting in its middle. He noticed the open shelter door.

"Damn!" he shouted. *"Vladimir!"*

Dravik ran back up the basement stairs, two steps per stride, straight into the waiting barrel of Officer Clayton's nine-millimeter. Behind Clayton, Vladimir, cuffed, was being taken to the bus.

"On your *knees*, Dravik!" shouted Clayton. "Hands on your head! You could have been *killed*, Taylor," Clayton said, "all *three* of you."

"I know, and please forgive us, sir. But we had to act. We *had* to."

"You did *not* ... Oh, hello," Clayton said. "I didn't see you standing there, but I *did* see you take down Vladimir as he was running. And you would be..."

"Hello. I'm a friend of Taylor's. Name's Sterling Vice."

Clayton shook Vice's hand. "Thanks for your help, Sterling Vice."

48

"Officer, can you tell us where this house's owner, Travis McGuire, might be," Rommy asked one in a group of FBI agents outside.

"McGuire? No one knows, son. Everything traceable about him has vanished, as far as we can tell. Credit card transactions, bills, fingerprints, nothing with any paper trail or DNA metrics, not even a hair. When did you last see him?"

CSI and FBI vehicles pulled onto the property's yard. Agents exited the vehicles and rushed into the house. Crowds of citizens, mumbling hushed, mouth-covered speculations, gathered on street corners and lawns. Taylor and Sterling walked from the house toward Rommy.

"What's going on now, Taylor?" Rommy asked.

Taylor sighed. "They've discovered the remains," she replied, handing Sterling his watch.

"Remains?"

"Of the five missing teens, apparently some of McGuire's *specimens*, maybe Dravik's. It's horrible. In the attic, stored in sealed freezers, hidden behind bricked spaces. Even the cadaver dogs missed it. McGuire, somebody, had used these kids for his transplantation experiments or organ-harvesting and had disposed of what he did not need in those freezers."

"Dear God," Bobbie said.

"Seems McGuire had been the *monster* of Raventon for all these years, hiding behind his facade of eccentricity, pretending to defend Miss Peasy and knowing such only *added* to the public's belief that, indeed, *she* was responsible for all the missing kids.

"Then along came Dravik and Vladimir. Pure coincidence they happened upon McGuire's ruse of preaching, his Crazy Travie persona. It fit their cover so conveniently."

"There are *no* coincidences," said Sterling. "Everything happens for a divine reason. What's more, they'll never find any biological trace of McGuire."

"Divine reasons sure work in mysterious ways," Bobbie said.

"In a very real and sinister sense, McGuire's mission *was* completed," Taylor said. "But not in a permanent sense. He did not possess Neal's watch. McGuire will forever after be known as the Monster of Raventon, and Miss Peasy is exonerated … permanently. Looks like your mission has won, Sterling."

"Won, perhaps, but not completed. There's still more to be done."

"Such as …" Rommy said.

"Get Miss Peasy's box of letters and such and take those items and deliver them directly into the hands of Cecil Adelman, at the Raventon Beacon. Cecil is their lifestyle writer and is an honest interpreter of history. Let journalism take its course. Her and her family's reputations and good names will be restored in due time.

"But the Raventon Beacon won't believe this anymore than I did," said Rommy. "How can they be convinced of this remarkable, divine truth?"

"Rommy has a point, Sterling," Taylor admitted. "If they're not convinced, the story either gets tossed into the waste bin of fantasy, or it serves to amplify the Witch of Raventon myth, even as this McGuire story is released."

"The parchment that my letters were written on, all of them, including the ones referencing Miss Peasy, are easily dated, through dating methodologies, to the Civil War period. The writing, too. The blood on my shirt, which I will give to you, contains essential DNA information linking me to the Sterling Vice of July 1863. Tests will prove it. Plus, while Confederate records show nothing of my service with any Southern regiment, as I was not officially mustered into any, and Confederate records are woefully incomplete, official records of the Union armies - they called it the War of the Rebellion - do contain my service at Gettysburg, including my wounding and capture and subsequent treatment and death in a Union field hospital … and the watch I hold here.

"Which brings me to this," Sterling said softly as he held the golden watch of Joseph O. Neal in his palm. He sighed and smiled, his eyes closed in remembrance. "There is no past; there is no future; there is only the present, and its ever-shifting gaggle of props and settings. God gives us those settings and guides us through them. Man is the keeper of Time, and God is the keeper of Man.

"Taylor … I want you to have this watch. God has blessed it with His divine power, for His divine purpose. Take it," he said, placing it in her hand and closing her fingers around it. "It is meant now for you. As Charlie said to me that tragic afternoon on a hot field at Gettysburg, 'take this watch; you'll need it. Trust me.'

"Now then," Sterling said, placing his hat on his head and then removing the hat, "there is someplace I have to be, if you'll excuse me."

Taylor smiled softly and squeezed her fingers tightly around the watch. A tear made its way down her cheek. Sterling Vice turned and started his walk down the street. He again placed his hat on his head, adjusting the hat's fit for the next phase of his incredible journey. He did not remove the hat, nor did he look back. Taylor, Bobbie, and Rommy watched Sterling, as the flurry of police activity continued its swirl around the McGuire house. Gradually, Sterling's form lightened, his body translucent, as it faded from view.

"Where's that Vice fellow," Officer Clayton asked as he made his way down the porch steps toward the Raventon Three. "I wanted to thank him once again."

"Vice?" Taylor said. "I'm … I'm not sure. He was just here. I'm sure we'll see him again."

49

Saturday morning
July 12, 2020, 8:22
Raventon Medical Center

"We came as soon as we heard, dad," Taylor said. "How's she doing?"

"Doesn't look good, sweetie."

"How long?"

" A minute; an hour …".

"Can we …?"

"Yes, you can see her. She's asked for the three of you."

Mike led the three down the hall to the elevator and up to room 417. They entered the room slowly, peeking around the half-opened door as they entered.

An oxygen mask was affixed to Miss Peasy's mouth. Intravenous lines fed into her right arm. Sheets and a blanket covered her to her chin.

She opened her eyes and turned her head slightly right. She produced a grin that typified the proud, conquering persona of Miss Peasy Parlevous.

"Hey, there, Taylor," she managed.

Taylor, Bobbie and Rommy walked to her bedside, tearful smiles on their faces.

"Hi, Miss Peasy," Taylor whispered. "What have you gone and gotten yourself into?"

Miss Peasy smiled. "I'm good, sweetie. Better'n I've ever been, thanks to you three and Sterling Vice … and God, of course.

"We need you out of here and back in your kitchen, baking us those unbeatable apple pies of yours," Taylor said. "I miss our tea times and your pipe, our conversations, and … I miss *you*, Miss Peasy."

"Maybe later. First things first. I have something for you."

Miss Peasy reached under her covers and pulled out Sterling Vice's bullet-shot Bible. She handed it to Taylor.

"Here," she said. "Sterling wanted you to have this. It's the symbol of life eternal, come what may. It supersedes time itself."

Taylor took the Bible, its life-taking bullet intact, stilled, inside its live-saving pages, and kissed Miss Peasy on her forehead.

"I've had a good life, Taylor, an …". Miss Peasy took a deep breath. "… an incredible life, a life that has surpassed all understanding. It's … been a blast, Taylor."

Taylor nodded. "Yes, ma'am, it has."

"And I am at peace. What … what time is it, on Sterling's pocket watch?"

Taylor retrieved the watch from her pocket. "8:43, Miss Peasy."

"Now the *real* fun can begin." Miss Peasy smiled. "Live your life just as well, Taylor, and … never surrender. Even when the odds … look rough."

Taylor smiled and sighed.

"Count on it. Thank you, Miss Peasy," she whispered, as Miss Peasy's fingers lay limp on Taylor's palm. "For letting me be a part. For *everything.* Rest now, sweet lady. I love you."

About the Author

Mark Randolph Watters is a native of Rome, Georgia and is now living in the Great Frozen North with his wife and daughter. He has authored five novels, seven children's picture books, and two volumes of short stories and poems. He was the winner of the Dahlonega (GA) Literary Festival Short Story Contest in 2005 and again in 2006.

Mark has been married for 33 years to a wonderfully loving and tolerant woman.

To preview all of Mark Randolph Watters' books, please go to the site links below.

http://www.lulu.com/spotlight/markwatters

http://kwp-books.com/

The Incredible Journey of Sterling Vice is **Book III** in the Raventon Mysteries series, featuring Taylor Smart. The first two titles are:

1) ***Taylor Smart and the Chamber of Skulls***
2) ***Blythington's Game***